This Thing
Called Love

This Thing Called Love

A MIRROR LAKE NOVEL

MIRANDA LIASSON

Montlake
Romance

Published by Montlake Romance, Seattle

www.apub.com

Amazon, the Amazon logo, and Montlake Romance are trademarks of Amazon.com, Inc., or its affiliates.

ISBN-13: 9781477829066
ISBN-10: 1477829067

Cover design by Shasti O'Leary-Soudant / SOS CREATIVE LLC

Library of Congress Control Number: 2014921457

Printed in the United States of America

For Ed, because you always knew I could.

CHAPTER 1

Olivia Marks steered her grocery cart to the back of the crowded twelve-items-or-less line just as her baby niece began to cry. Wedged in her car seat between several bottles of diet cola, a jar of peanut butter, two frozen pizzas, a head of lettuce, and one roll of refrigerated cookie dough, Annabelle looked defenseless and diminutive. And mad as hell.

Olivia surreptitiously dropped two Kit Kat bars into the cart. She had to get out of this store before the crying really got rolling. Annabelle waved her arms and wailed as loud as an EMS vehicle on the way to the ER, the very picture of despair. Olivia felt her pain. She had the same feeling bubbling up inside herself right now.

People cast accusatory looks in her direction. *Do something about that crying. What kind of mother are you?* All around, people bustled about Gertie's in their usual routines, but for Olivia, nothing was usual. Her life had changed faster than a Black Friday crowd rushing into Walmart, and she wasn't at all prepared. She didn't belong here, back under the microscope lens of her small hometown with a brand new baby she knew nothing about caring for.

The crying suddenly accelerated to tornado-warning pitch. Everyone turned and stared. Olivia counted eight people in front of her in line. Eight!

If only the older woman who had stopped to admire Annabelle in the vegetable aisle hadn't clanged her necklace against the cart and woken her up, this nightmare wouldn't be happening.

A silent prayer rose to Olivia's lips. *Just let me get my peanut butter home.* Olivia's stomach rumbled in response. How long had it been since she'd eaten?

Breakfast felt like a hundred years ago. The day had been a rush of meetings and loose ends too numerous to count. Then she'd rented a car and driven the two and a half hours from New York City to Connecticut, to her best friend Alex's, to pick up the four-week-old baby.

"Shhh, Annabelle, shush." She held the baby's tiny hand. It was so weightless—fragile—that Olivia pushed down a tide of panic. "Just a little while longer." She sounded like she was begging, not comforting.

A wave of helplessness engulfed her. *Helpless* was not a word she ever would have used to describe herself. Her job as an editor of self-help books at Andromeda Publishing in the city meant eighty-hour workweeks, high-pressure deadlines, and six-figure deals. But a *baby* . . . that was a whole other can of worms. One she had never expected to factor into her well-ordered life.

Her heart squeezed painfully as she recalled the car accident that had claimed the lives of her sister Trish and brother-in-law Kevin. They'd gone out to the garden center to buy more flowers for their tiny yard. On a Saturday afternoon, in broad daylight, a drunk driver had crossed the median, killing them instantly. Accordion-pleated the entire front half of the car as easily as a teenage boy would flatten a Coke can between his hands. Yet miraculously, the tiny baby had survived, tucked and buckled into her car seat in the back.

Desperation and despair threatened to thrash up inside Olivia like breaker waves over rocks, pummeling her and threatening to break her into a million pieces. Yet she was strangely numb, fueled by adrenaline and caffeine, and mercifully distracted by the impossible responsibility she'd been called upon to bear.

The interceding week had been a blur of packing, rearranging her schedule, her commitments, her *life* . . . to return home and take guardianship of Annabelle as her sister's and brother-in-law's wills had dictated.

Olivia set her jaw firmly and pushed down all the sadness, fears, and doubts that churned about inside her. Like why Trish had named her, the most unlikely of people, to take on such a critical job.

No, she wasn't going there, to that dark place. Annabelle deserved better, and Olivia was determined, for Trish's sake, to do whatever it took to give her baby the best life possible. She owed it to her sister, and to Annabelle, because that's what Olivia always did. Her best. Always.

A middle-aged woman behind her whispered to her companion, "That's why I never took mine out till they were six months old. Babies that age belong at home."

If only she had a pacifier. With chagrin, Olivia remembered she'd left the diaper bag Alex had packed for her in the car.

"So disruptive," the other woman said with a *tsk*.

Why had she ever thought to bring the baby grocery shopping? It was only that she didn't want to ask anyone for help on her first day back. Anything she could do herself, she usually did. Asking for help was never her forte.

Of all the self-help books she'd edited and read, no well-meaning advice seemed to leap into her head for this situation. *Meditate. Think positive. Send calming vibes into the universe. Avoid clutter.* All useless in the face of a screaming, inconsolable infant.

She wracked her brain. What else could she do to calm Annabelle? *Rocking motion.* She'd seen mothers do that with good results. Olivia began to roll the cart back and forth in what she thought was a soothing rhythm. "There you go, Annie. It's all right, baby. Just a few more minutes."

Something *dinged.* Olivia looked up to see a flashing light on top of the cashier's station.

God, no. Not the help light.

The cashier barked into a microphone, "Price check needed at register seven. Price check. Register seven."

Olivia shifted her weight from one foot to another. She still wore her heels, and right about now, her toes were screaming for flip-flops. She cracked her neck to dispel some tension, then bent low to whisper, "Four more people, Annie. You can do it."

Annabelle's cries intensified to all-out wails. Her face turned reddish-purple as a beet, her tiny mouth contorted into a vibrating oval.

That was the white flag of surrender. Olivia would have to take the plunge and pick her up.

People stared, judgment written on their faces. Hadn't anyone ever seen a baby cry before? She undid the belt between Annabelle's tiny flailing legs and lifted her out of the car seat.

"What's that awful smell?" someone from the next aisle looked over and said.

What sm—It soon became evident that the diaper had clearly leaked, leaving poo strewn all over the car seat and halfway up Annabelle's back. The sensation of wetness covered Olivia's hands and arms. She gulped and drew one hand away to find it covered with something she didn't even want to vocalize.

A groan escaped her lips. A cowardly image flashed through her mind of setting the baby back down and fleeing as far and fast as she could.

She awkwardly bounced the squawking baby.

I would never abandon you, Annabelle. Because I know what that's like. And you will never experience that. Ever. Instinctively, she held the baby more securely. Trish might have been too young to remember when their own mother left, but Olivia remembered it like it was yesterday. Remembered all too clearly the betrayal and shock of knowing your own mother did not love you enough to stay.

A man on the other side of her chuckled. The lady behind her folded her arms and muttered, "I'm complaining to the manager about this."

Olivia scanned the crowd. Wasn't there another mom in sight? Someone, anyone to lend a hand? She was one away from the cashier, but how on earth was she ever going to check out? But put the groceries back? Impossible. She'd have to abandon them. What could possibly be more embarrassing?

Behind her, she heard the rattle of groceries being shifted about. What was that awful woman up to now?

Olivia spun about, ready to give her something much bigger to complain about, like a roll of cookie dough lodged somewhere unmentionable, but the woman was no longer in line.

In her place stood a man, tall and lean. The muscles of his back pulled gently against the confines of a crisp white shirt as he rummaged through his cart. Rolled-up sleeves displayed tan, well-built arms. Perfectly tailored dress pants clung to a fine backside and looked made just for him.

Hottie plucked out a roll of paper towels and turned. Olivia took one look at his face and gasped.

No, it couldn't be. Not here, not like this. Anytime but now.

She recognized the same arrogantly cocked brow, as if he'd sized her up after ten-plus years and found her way below his exacting standards. The same square-set jaw: hard, obstinate, and unyielding. The same bright, piercing eyes: as pale green as sea foam and as displeased as Grandma when you forgot to wash behind the ears.

She used to cut his wavy mop of hair because he could never afford haircuts. But now it was shorn close to his head, dark and coarse and dangerous, a little closer on the sides than the top. A haircut he'd clearly shelled out a bunch for.

The contrast between the boy he was and the man he'd become sent a prick of remorse through her. Half of her wanted to rush to him, be gathered up in his strong arms like when she was a girl, while the other jaded half knew only too well exactly how much had changed.

A graphic silk tie and Italian leather shoes completed his male model look and reminded her he was a bajillionaire by now. Entrepreneur, owner of five Zagat-rated restaurants, with another rumored to open soon. What was he even doing in a grocery store, when he had minions to do such a mundane task?

"Brad," she said on an exhale. She followed the movement of his long-fingered hands, sliding up his muscular arms before she could stop herself. Her gaze locked with those unusual green eyes that held a trace of amusement and something more—a mocking that suddenly turned her blood to ice. It reminded her that on the outside, this man might look as bright and charismatic as a poison dart frog but he was toxic as all get-out.

"Olivia," he said matter-of-factly, in a tone that guaranteed he'd been watching her for some time. He offered her a bunch of paper towels.

She wished anyone else would have been handing them to her. Why Brad Rushford, her first crush, her first love, the one person she did *not* want to see with all her defenses down?

Oh, but she'd better get used to it. She'd be seeing him plenty. He was Annabelle's uncle, Kevin's brother, and the one person who shared the commonality of this tragedy with her in exactly the same way. Whether she liked it or not, he was back in her life. And he did not look happy *she* had been the one named Annabelle's guardian.

Her sister had been married to Brad's brother, Kevin. Her best friend Alex was married to his next-youngest brother, Tom. And her other best friend, Meg, had a years-long crush on the youngest brother, Benjamin. Good thing Olivia had fled a town where everyone she knew thought the Rushford brothers were the only eligible men around.

They most certainly weren't. But they were the most good-looking. She took the towels, trying her best not to snatch them in irritation. "Th-thank you." *Dammit*, she'd stumbled over her words like a high school girl on a first date. It was only the baby's screaming, the exhaustion, the horrendous stress throwing her off her game.

"Looks like you could use some help."

It wasn't a nice offer. Olivia could tell from the know-it-all tone and skeptical spark in his eyes that Brad was furious. He'd told his brother Tom, and then of course Alex had told her, that Olivia having custody was the worst mistake. He didn't believe she was suitable to be a mother.

For a second, her doubt, her pain, all her insecurities crowded tightly around her like a ring of horrible bullies on the playground. He of all people knew her history better than anyone. It hurt that someone she was once so close to would judge her like that.

But maybe he was right.

Olivia's stomach churned sickly but she braced herself. She was too old to care what Brad Rushford thought. He was a part of her past and she could easily keep him locked away there.

Except he smelled good, like spicy, woodsy cologne. And he was so much taller and more filled out than he'd been twelve years ago, when they were in high school. He was eye candy, the deep, dark-chocolate variety.

Twelve years ago. Something flashed in her head. The strangest memory. They'd gone parking on the back roads of the local airport just outside of town. In Brad's beat-up old clunker, it was pitch-black except for the glow from the cool blue lights lined up along the runways in the distance.

The night air was bitingly cold, yet everything in that tiny car was hot. Rain beat loudly on the roof, encasing them with the muted noise, and their breath steamed the windows, creating the perfect curtain of privacy. Kiss after wet, languid kiss covered her lips until at last his tongue collided and tangled with hers, sending the sensation of shooting stars bursting through her and making her quiver all over.

Brad's youthful face hovered over hers, so close, those pale green eyes brimming with intensity and lust and something she had been certain once upon a time was love. "Let me make love to you," he said, his voice solemn and worshipful and thrilling her to the core.

It wasn't their first time, but they were still tentative, still learning each other's bodies. He made love to her so carefully, with such restraint, she'd had to tell him she was *fine, just fine.* They'd let loose together, uninhibited, free flying to heights she'd never experienced with anyone in all the time since. "I love you, Olivia," he'd said in a hoarse whisper. "I swear I'll love you forever."

Under the cold fluorescent lighting of Gertie's, Olivia shook her head, pulled her libido and her sentimentality back in line. For a second she'd forgotten she was still in the middle of a grocery store checkout with a miserable, freaking-out baby and angry customers.

Brad tossed out a cocky smile. *Shit*, he'd seen her ogling him. She had to be more careful, not display her emotions so flagrantly, or he would surely pounce on any weakness she presented.

In her business life, she was used to handling aggressive men who tried to one-up her on big deals all the time. Usually by dishing it right back.

"Always glad to rescue a damsel in distress." Brad dangled another paper towel from his fingers. She wanted to use it to wipe the smug grin right off his face.

Instead, she placed it on Annabelle's back.

"Thanks, Brad." Olivia smiled sweetly. "But I don't need anyone coming to my rescue—especially not the man from Brawny."

CHAPTER 2

Brad couldn't help chuckling despite the mini-crisis before him. Olivia always had possessed the power to get his hormones rolling, and today was no exception, standing there with her big melted-chocolate eyes, like one of those long-lashed dolls his four-year-old niece played with that looked flirty and innocent at the same time.

But neither of them was innocent anymore. Tragedy had intervened and torn a hole in their lives. His brother was gone, and this tiny baby was the only reminder he would ever have of him. Securing her future was all that mattered. And he would go to his grave doing it.

Still, an unwanted warmth surged through him and shot straight to his groin. He fought the urge to tug the clips out of her crazy curly hair and plow his hands through it. Luxuriate in the silky mass that he knew would be soft as a baby's skin. Kiss her full pink lips senseless.

Brad struggled to squelch the lust factor. He'd known her when she was naïve and innocent. Hell, he had been, too. But together they'd made fireworks. Big, bold, Technicolor ones. Like out on the lake in that old fishing boat, a flannel blanket tossed over his backside for anyone who happened to be strolling by on that moon-filled night. He'd been up on his elbows in that cramped little boat, looking down at the most beautiful girl he'd ever seen. "I want you so badly," he'd choked out.

She'd looked at him without hesitation. Those big brown eyes had glistened with feeling, making him tremble like he couldn't control himself. She was beautiful, perfect, and her absolute surrender made him want to protect her forever. "I love you," she'd whispered, her body arched against him.

She had cracked his tough shell for the first time in all the hard years of his eighteen-year-old life. For that brief spot of time, the burdens he'd carried for his family had lifted, and his heart burst wide open, naked and vulnerable.

Stupid, stupid. Damned old memories from a million years ago, stirred up from where they should have stayed, dust-covered and undisturbed. She'd caught him off guard, that was all. Lack of sex would do that to a man and he would take steps to rectify that immediately.

He'd known she was coming back to get the baby but he never expected to run into her like this, in Gertie's, with Annabelle all worked up and Olivia at her wit's end trying to console her.

He'd hung back as long as he could, but he was never good at doing nothing. It was in his nature to jump in and help. Despite knowing he shouldn't.

Because Annabelle belonged here, in Mirror Lake, with her family. Her *whole* family. Not in New York City with a single career woman who dragged herself exhausted into her apartment after a twelve-hour workday with barely enough energy to pull a take-out menu off her refrigerator door and call for dinner.

So Brad would help, but it wouldn't be for Olivia's sake. No siree. "Hey, Annie," he cooed, patting the baby on the back. "Easy there, honey." If he'd thought the familiarity of his voice would soothe her, he was wrong. She was beyond consolation. His legendary finesse with women clearly didn't work on his baby niece.

"Here you go." He reached over with more towels, urging Olivia to place them between Annabelle's butt and her hand.

Olivia glanced up and nodded, all jesting tossed aside with the baby's heightened cries. A quick skim of a look, but it pricked his heart with a mixture of sadness and vulnerability that made him feel something he absolutely did not want to feel. Once upon a time he would have turned somersaults to urge some laughter back into those soulful brown eyes.

But not now.

She'd left him once, and once was enough, thank you very much. Okay, so maybe he'd encouraged her to go but he'd had no choice. A full scholarship to NYU had been her ticket to sail, whereas he'd stayed behind, anchored down with the hefty task of raising three feisty younger brothers and a sister.

Everything she'd experienced—international friends, foods, theater shows and art, different ways of thinking and dressing and acting—seemed foreign to him. Served to magnify their differences and his insecurities, and in the end he couldn't handle it. He'd felt unworthy and she'd just . . . changed.

The Olivia in front of him was not the same person he once knew. She looked so sophisticated, in her fancy blouse and high heels. She'd been a pretty girl but now she was a stunning woman, and everything about her spelled success. A city girl through and through, far removed from their tiny tourist town.

"I can take her," he offered.

"No!" she said adamantly. "I-I'm almost at checkout."

Figured she would refuse his help. That much hadn't changed.

Olivia always was determined to do everything on her own. From fiercely studying for college placement tests to raising the most money ever for the children's cancer drive she'd organized senior year.

She'd rarely been back home since she got that high-up job somewhere in the publishing industry. Except for briefly at the funeral, he hadn't seen her since the day Trish married his younger brother.

Yet they'd picked her, not him, to mother their child. And he knew why, too. Because he sucked at child rearing. At least he'd been fifteen, not a baby, when he'd lost his parents. He'd basically raised all four of his siblings through the nightmare of their teen years by himself, and he'd made mistakes. Did his best holding down three jobs and taking college classes at night, but things were far from perfect.

All the more reason for him to fight tooth and nail for his dead brother's child. And he *would* fight for this helpless baby to get the *best* life, the life she deserved, with a proper family who loved her more than life itself. Two loving people who would move heaven and earth for her happiness and security.

And he had just the right two people in mind. His brother Tom and his wife Alex already had three little kids and enough love between them to share with at least one more. They'd already kept Annabelle for the past week. All he had to do was convince them that keeping her permanently was the best decision for everyone.

"Got a pacifier?" he asked.

"In the car."

"Suppose the bottle's there, too."

Could nodding be sexy? Because it was when she did it.

The cashier leaned over the black conveyer belt. "You two lovebirds are next!"

Brad winced. *Lord, that was so long ago.* Couldn't anyone in this town forget anything? "Can it, Gertie," Brad scolded the gray-haired woman behind the register. "Can't you see we need a little help here?"

"Just hand over a credit card, Bradley, and you can give 'em all the help in the world on your own time." Gertie cracked her gum and leaned her ample floral-shirt-covered bosom farther over the belt. "Hi, Olivia. Long time no see, sugar."

"Hey, Gertie," Olivia managed weakly.

"C'mon, lady, let's get the line moving," someone heckled. Olivia's face flamed. She spun around to address a stocky man at the back of the line in a plaid shirt, worn jeans, and work boots. "I thought that in Mirror Lake, people were actually polite to one another." Brad bit back a smile. She still possessed her same spunk, and it was more appealing than ever.

"That applies to people who don't let their babies scream for twenty minutes, lady. You're a public menace."

Brad frowned and turned around. "Mike, is that you? Surely you wouldn't be giving Annabelle's aunt trouble."

"Oh, hey, Brad." The man's tone suddenly turned contrite. "You know this woman?"

Brad nodded. "My niece's aunt. Mind your manners."

Brad looked at Olivia. *Big mistake.* For a second an expression that might have been gratefulness passed over her features, softening them and making her even more gorgeous. He hadn't realized he was staring until she met his gaze and blushed, just as aware of the snap of electricity between them as he was.

Well, he'd had to say *something.* No one should talk to a woman like that. He would've stood up for anyone.

"That Kevin's kid?" Mike asked. "I'm sorry, man. I had no idea. Can I help?"

Brad winced at the mention of his deceased brother's name, but forced himself to focus on Olivia and Annabelle. He took hold of Olivia's arm. Just a light touch, at the crook of her elbow. Her skin was petal soft and for the first time he noticed she smelled like those tiny white flowers his grandma grew on the shady side of the white clapboard house where he'd grown up. He lowered his voice, spoke only to her. "Why don't you take the baby out to the car while I get the groceries?"

"Just let me give you my credit ca—" She looked frantically in the cart, checked both her shoulders for a strap.

"Oh no. My purse—"

"Where did you last have it?" Brad asked.

"I moved it after she woke up . . . veggie aisle. Near the grapes. It's probably gone by now—"

"I'll get her purse," Mike said.

"Thanks, buddy." Brad cracked a half grin and turned to Olivia. "He's not so bad once you get on his good side."

Brad unloaded the groceries and handed Gertie a credit card, which she took with a subdued nod. "Want me to make an announcement about the purse?" she asked.

"Maybe just send Sam over to watch the doors in case anyone tries to leave with it. Mind if I grab another thing or two real quick?"

She expelled a heavy sigh. "You are pushing me today, young man."

"I'll be right back." Before Olivia could protest that he'd paid for her groceries, he turned and sprinted down an aisle. He could hear Annabelle's cries behind him, loud and clear and strong.

He returned a moment later, gesturing to Gertie and holding up three more items that she scanned quickly.

After he signed the receipt, Brad found Olivia near the exit and steered her to two plastic chairs near the store's front office. He quickly ripped the cardboard off a baby bottle. Next he took a bottle of water, uncapped it, and rinsed off the bottle and nipple, pouring the excess into a geranium plant nearby. Then he popped a formula can open and poured it into the bottle. Ten seconds later, the bottle was in Annabelle's mouth.

And quiet was restored.

Olivia's face flooded with relief. Curlicues of hair sprung from her bun to frame her face. Her clothes were wrinkled, and he couldn't help but notice her blouse had come a little more open on top than usual, allowing him a glimpse of a sweet curve of cleavage and something pretty and lacy underneath.

He mentally smacked himself. Here he was thinking of sex when all Olivia's focus was on Annabelle, who sucked urgently, caring only about satisfying her hunger.

Odd, but at that moment, Olivia looked more beautiful than he'd ever remembered. Maybe it was all the sadness of these past few weeks that made him so sentimental. Or needy. Because he suddenly wanted to be eighteen again, feeling that frantic desperation that had them making love in canoes and under trees and once on a blanket on a dewy hillside under a full moon overlooking the lake. For a flash, he was back in the past, when things were simple and he was so damn in love with her.

Olivia rubbed her forehead against her shoulder to push the hair from her face. She exhaled a big breath and smiled. "Thank you."

That high-wattage smile was sincere and honest and for some strange reason, it punched Brad right in the gut.

But he was not going to let her get to him. Annabelle was his niece and he was not about to allow Big City Girl to flounce into town and take her away from all the family she had. To a metropolitan life full of nannies and an absent mother who cared more about her career than anything else.

Mike ran up the aisle carrying Olivia's shoulder bag. "Purse found in aisle two."

Olivia accepted it, exhaling a pent-up breath. "Oh, thanks."

"Hey, it's all right. And I'm sorry I harassed you earlier. Any friend of Brad's is a friend of mine." He extended a hand, then recoiled and put it in his pocket. "I'd shake your hand, but . . ."

"Not today, I understand." Olivia's mouth tilted up in not quite a smile.

As he left the store, Olivia asked, "Who is that guy, anyway?"

"Mike restores old homes. He's working on a bunch of the old Victorians on the square." Her cool-headed gaze rose to meet his, and she studied him thoroughly for the first time. Damn those wide brown eyes, expressive and honest and wary. For a second he felt that dangerous spark she'd always incited in him, clear through to his toes. It did something crazy to him, making him blurt, "Can I drive you home?"

Brad winced. Why had he just asked that? *Be helpful, but keep your distance,* a stern voice in his head warned. Why couldn't he do that, even after all these years and all that muddied-up water under their bridge?

"Do you mind?" *That* was unexpected. She was actually accepting help? *Of course he minded.* This was not good. That same powerful force field of attraction drew him to her like a magnet, threatening to take his composure and shatter it like a baseball through glass.

Action. He needed action to take his mind off this crazy spell she cast on him. So he jumped up, grabbed the cart of groceries. Red police car sirens flashed inside his head. Olivia wasn't just an old girlfriend, she'd become family the moment her sister had married his brother. She was someone he would have to interact with on some level for the rest of his life because of their connection to Annabelle.

Throwing sex into that mix was like dating your boss. Never a good idea.

Grateful for some distance to clear his head, Brad pushed the cart with the groceries outside while Olivia carried Annabelle. He opened Olivia's rental car door with her key while she snapped Annabelle's car seat onto its base. Olivia slid in beside Annabelle, not daring to take the bottle out of her mouth.

He got in and drove. The familiar landmarks of their small town passed by—the tall steeple of the Congregational church, the old theater, the bed and breakfast with its wrap-around porch and baskets of hanging ferns. The hardware store Olivia's father owned. Pie in the Sky, the old diner with its neon sign that had been a favorite hangout in high school.

The tiny downtown was quaint as a postcard, but to Brad it was just home, a place he'd lived every day of his life. Bound in with his blood and bones, and therefore not usually contemplated. Yet he couldn't help wondering what memories it stirred for her.

That big pine tree on the square by the gazebo where he'd first kissed her. The canoe they'd often used to paddle out onto the lake from his grandmother's house on balmy summer nights. Sitting on the porch swing under his grandma's watchful eye.

And that red brick Victorian on the corner with the big side yard and that turret, where they'd snuck in one fine spring evening.

Back then, he hadn't been out to conquer one woman after the next. He'd dreamt of forever.

Fool boy that he was. What did he know?

Too late, Rushford. Ten years too late. Let it go. Bygones and all that.

Brad broke out of reminiscing and looked in the rearview mirror, to find Olivia staring at him. She quickly looked away. "Town look the same to you?" He kept his tone casual.

Olivia nodded. "This part of it, anyway."

"Hasn't changed much on the outside, but on the inside it has."

"What do you mean?"

"Well, it's grown up. Become more tourist-conscious. The marina's gotten built up the last couple of years and the downtown's opened up more specialty stores and restaurants for visitors who want to stroll and shop."

"I'm glad to hear it's prospering."

He had a sudden urge to point out his own restaurant on the marina, nearly done being renovated. His baby, his pride and joy.

Too personal. He kept the conversation light until he drove the mile and a half to an old neighborhood of century-old homes and pulled up to a tiny craftsman-style house with a low-gabled roof and fat columns holding up a covered front porch.

"Thanks for the ride," Olivia said.

Brad stepped out and opened the back door. Olivia unhooked the baby's seat and Brad lifted it out. Annabelle sat in a relaxed slump, completely passed out from exhaustion.

Together they crunched up the gravel driveway to the front door.

He paused while she rummaged inside her bag for the key. Her hand shook as she placed it in the lock and turned the knob.

She glanced up at him briefly as the door opened. Uncertainty and doubt flashed over her face before she could neutralize her expression. He knew what she was thinking, *felt* her thinking it. She was on her own, in her sister's old house, being a parent for the first time. All on a week's notice.

Suddenly he felt as lost as she did. She of all people understood the shock of losing someone you loved. That fact had changed both their lives and would bind them forever, regardless of the anger he felt over her getting the baby.

"Well, thanks so much for helping me." Olivia steeled her shoulders, snapped her professional mask carefully into place. "Annabelle and I . . . really appreciate it. I'll make certain to reimburse you for the groceries."

Brad waved his hand in dismissal. "It's the least I can do. Do you need anything?" *Dammit, there he went again.* Didn't he even have the sense not to stand too close to the flame in case it burned him again?

"Just a much-needed bath—both of us." She gestured toward her clothes.

Yeah. The heat flared again, ready to singe at any moment. Images flashed through his head that had no business there. Involving her gorgeous curves soaking in a tub full of bubbles.

Brad stepped back, grasping frantically for rational thought. "What's your plan with Annabelle?" he blurted, mostly to douse the hormones flying rampantly between them.

Olivia curved a brow in surprise but answered calmly. "I've got two weeks off. It was all my boss could spare. I'm nearing a deadline with a big author and he can't be kept waiting much longer."

"I see. Then you're taking her back to the City?"

She nodded. "That would be the most reasonable plan."

"But is it the best plan for her?"

Remorse pricked him as he watched delicate lines appear between her eyes. He didn't want to be an ass but there was no pretending he felt peachy about this.

"What do you mean?"

"Well, you're single, aren't you?"

"Lots of people are."

"And you work a lot, right?"

Olivia shook her head. "I'm not getting into this with you. Thanks for the ride, Brad." She walked through the doorway but he stepped up and prevented her from shutting the door.

"All I'm saying is, Annabelle's whole family is here in Mirror Lake. If you take her away, you take her away from all of us. Is that really what you want?"

She set the carrier down and poked a manicured finger into his chest. "If your idea of raising a child is for a mom to abandon her business suits for a red-checkered apron and bake cherry pies all day long, you are living on Sexist Idiot Planet Number Nine. There are all kinds of mothers and, from what I've seen, you're no expert."

"I am an expert, sweetness." The hairs on his neck bristled. Was she criticizing the job he'd done with his siblings? Every minute of raising them had been worry and torture, something he never wanted to tackle again. "I know it takes a lot of sacrifice and delaying gratification. Something you might not know with your big city life."

"You know nothing about me or my 'big city life.'" She handed him her keys and addressed him over her shoulder. "You can take my car home. I'll get it back later."

"Don't need to."

She spun back around. "What?"

"That's my house right there."

Olivia's head snapped up to follow the direction of his outstretched arm. Another old house, similar to its neighbor, sat surrounded by a tidy white picket fence.

"You're kidding."

He shot her a big Cheshire grin. The outrage on her face told him she knew he wasn't.

"Trish never told me you lived next door."

Those big brown eyes tossed daggers at him. She was mad as hell. Once upon a time, he'd been on the receiving end of all that zest for life. Strangely, his anger ebbed, replaced by a sudden hard yearning that socked him out of nowhere. He wanted to bask in all that vitality and passion that stroked him in all the wrong places.

It was one hell of a turn-on.

Instead, he stepped away. "Kevin gave me a heads-up when he found out their neighbor was moving and I made an offer. The deal just came through after . . . after the funeral. It's only temporary until I find a bigger place." Maybe one of those big Victorians on the square, tall and proud and neglected. He didn't mind putting in the work and it would be good for the town, too.

"I see." Her voice was total Popsicles. An awkward silence filled the space between them. "Well, thanks again."

Olivia clearly wasn't pleased. Well, neither was he. His baby sister, Samantha, was finally in college and his grandma had just moved to assisted living. For the first time in his life, he was free, and he wasn't about to ruin that freedom by dredging up some long-lost love affair from high school. Especially when his niece's happiness lay on the line.

Olivia wasn't the same girl he knew. And he wasn't sure he liked the woman, no matter how many other parts of his anatomy still did.

He had two weeks to secure Annabelle's future. And to get Olivia to do the right thing. If that meant having the self-control to keep his hands off her, so be it. With all the arguing they'd just done, it should be easy.

Then why did he have the feeling he was in for two of the longest weeks of his life?

CHAPTER 3

"Dad?" Olivia shuffled groggily across the kitchen and fumbled to unlock the door. Bright spring sunlight shined in wide golden beams across the refinished wood floor. As she flipped the latch, she glanced at the boxy clock with a big gold pendulum hanging on Trish's wall. *Seven a.m.* She'd been up three times with Annabelle during the night and her bones ached to collapse back into bed. Her head felt like she'd had one too many drinks the night before except without any memories of having fun. Olivia peeled her tongue off the roof of her dry, pasty mouth and managed a smile for her father, who crossed the threshold to envelop her in his burly arms.

"What are you doing here so early?" Olivia asked. It was the first time she'd seen him since the funeral. That thought blew in a rush of others, scattered and brittle as fall leaves despite the inflow of balmy air that promised a beautiful May day.

Guilt pierced Olivia as she admitted she hadn't exactly seen her dad—really *visited* with him—in a long time. Trish had been the good daughter. The one who moved back after college and worked in town as a librarian. Who had time to volunteer and sit on committees and plant a garden and spend time with their aging father. Olivia had been far too busy building her career to spend much time in Mirror Lake.

And, to be honest, Mirror Lake, this lovely, quaint "Hometown for America," as the town motto proclaimed, held a cache of painful memories, of her mother and of Brad. Olivia had avoided coming home for a long time. But now Trish was gone. Her dad deserved a better daughter. But how could she ever fill the void that Trish had left?

"Hi, Livvy." Frank Marks gave his daughter a big squeeze and placed a kiss on top of her head. His greeting was cheery but the smile didn't quite reach his eyes, signs of the stress the last few weeks had brought. "Bill Daniels came by the store and said he saw your lights on early this morning, so I thought I'd stop by." He waved a white bakery bag in front of her nose. The smells of cinnamon and fresh dough invaded Olivia's nostrils, made her mouth water.

"Cinnamon rolls? From Mona's?" Olivia couldn't help smiling as she peeked into the bag at the special treat. Every Saturday morning for years, her dad had brought them home and she and Trish would roll out of bed to devour them before he went off to work. He claimed it was a way to get them up and doing their Saturday chores.

What he didn't know is that they usually dove straight back into bed afterward, but always rushed to get the chores done by early afternoon when he returned. Neither wanted to disappoint the man who worked tirelessly to be both a mom and a dad to them.

"I would've brought coffee, too, but I figured you'd already have some on. Brought you the paper, though." He pulled a rubber band off the rolled newspaper and set it on the kitchen island.

Olivia, more awake now, opened cupboard doors. Trish and Kevin had beautified the old kitchen with dark craftsman-style cabinets, golden-veined granite, and modern-looking pendant lights over the island with pretty green, blue, and red glass shades. Trish had always had an exquisite sense of decor. For the thousandth time, an ache split her heart. She knew her dad must be thinking of them, too.

"No coffee." Olivia couldn't keep the dismay out of her voice as she stood on tiptoe to view the top shelf of a corner cupboard. The thought of going back to the grocery store made her shudder. She found two small pottery plates and set them on the small island. Her father was already sitting, reading the paper.

"Shouldn't you be at work?" she asked as she plunged her hand into the bakery bag and took out a warm roll, tore a small piece off the end and popped it in her mouth. *Heaven.* She hadn't eaten anything this decadent in ages.

"Charlie's watching the store. We don't open till eight anyway." Olivia couldn't remember a weekday when her dad hadn't shown up at Mirror Lake Hardware by seven. "Heard you had a little problem in Gertie's yesterday." Her dad's eyebrows raised inquisitively over the top of the paper.

"Who told you that?" *Uh oh.* If her dad knew, so did everybody else.

"About ten or so people who came into the store yesterday afternoon."

Olivia groaned. "Annabelle just got a little fussy." No sense in going into detail. The only time a person had a moment of privacy in this town was on the commode. And even that wasn't guaranteed.

"Heard Brad Rushford helped you out."

Just the mention of Brad's name made her heart skitter. Stupid muscle memory. "He did," she said in a tone she hoped sounded nonchalant. She left out the part about her hands being covered with baby poo and the fact that she'd lost her purse.

Her dad looked at her good and hard over the top of his bifocals. "I know you'll be running into him now and again—"

"Dad, he lives *next door.*"

Dead silence. "Well, like I said, you'll see him occasionally, but that doesn't mean—"

Olivia stretched her arm across the island to cover her dad's hand with hers. "Brad was a long time ago. We've both moved on."

Her father set the paper down, making it crinkle loudly. "He's dated a lot of women and from what I've heard, he'll be cherry-picking as long as there's fruit in season."

"Dad!" He was always big into metaphors but . . . really. Still, her father was right. Brad had it all—brains, money, looks—and, apparently, the pick of the orchard.

"Heard he's doing some sort of bachelor cooking competition at his restaurant over the Memorial Day weekend and the women in town are all riled up about it. I don't want you to be another notch on his bedpost."

"Okay, enough already." Olivia felt her cheeks heat like she was fifteen years old.

"I just don't want to see you hurt again." Brad had been a huge blip on her screen of life, and her father had seen the explosive attraction and the devastating end. No wonder he was wary.

Brad had been everything to her—kind-hearted, hardworking, and sexy as sin, and she'd loved him with all her eighteen-year-old heart. Yet life had an uncanny way of playing "Gotcha!" She'd wanted that scholarship to NYU since she was twelve years old and learned what editors did to the books she'd treasured, but the day she got it, she'd cried tears of anguish.

Something deep inside her knew that going to New York would be the end for them. How could it not? In many ways, Brad's future was held prisoner by the needs of his family, and hers had no limits.

Her father had spoken like Brad was still a threat. Olivia wanted to assure him he most definitely was not. "Last night he was just helping out."

Her dad shot her a skeptical look, but he remained silent. Then he slid back his stool, indicating the conversation had ended. "The baby's all right?"

Olivia nodded. "Eats a full bottle then crashes like a lumberjack." Too bad the crash part only lasted a couple hours at a time.

"And how about you? Caring for an infant on your own is exhausting." He stood and neatly folded the paper, left it in a tidy pile.

Olivia, lacking a napkin, ran the back of her hand over her mouth and licked at a cinnamon gob on her lower lip. It was impossible to be neat with anything from Mona's. She sighed. "I don't know, Dad. My boss gave me two weeks' leave to figure it out. I've always dreamed of being a mother someday, but not like this."

Her father patted her forearm. "Life sometimes throws us curveballs. But you have to stay in the box and swing away."

He'd been doing that—gently patting, prodding, and delivering platitudes—since the day her mother left when she was nine years old. Raised two girls all on his own. How had he done it, when taking care of one tiny baby felt like scaling Everest without an oxygen tank?

Words pushed against her throat, demanding exit, but she choked them down. *Why me?* She wanted to know. *Why did Trish pick me?* But her father was doing his usual comforting in the face of his own grief— how could she demand more?

Honestly, Olivia feared her father's answer. It might be something funny, like *beats the hell out of me,* or something practical, like *don't know but you'll have to make the best of it,* but she was certain it wouldn't be *because you're the natural choice.*

She knew she wasn't. She'd always thought of having babies as some pleasant, distant event, way *way* in the future . . . not today, catching her off guard with her breeches at her knees.

Olivia would never do what her mother had done—make promises she couldn't keep. Promise this baby a life and then leave her. No, Olivia would do what she always did—assess the situation, examine her options, and do what was best for Annabelle. She owed that much to Trish.

Sensing her confusion, her dad continued his pep talk. "I raised you to be resourceful and figure out how to help yourself, and by God, you have."

Yes, she had, that's what she'd done, but far away from here. Guilt pummeled her. Truth was, she'd always felt a ferocious need to flee, to make a success out of her life far away from Mirror Lake. She didn't want to remember the failures—not being good enough that her own mother would stay and care for her. And not good enough for Brad.

Her father smiled. He'd always just loved her. Period. "I'm glad you're here, Livvy, and I know you'll figure out how to make this work. Just a shame it took something like this to bring you back."

She gave her father a sideways hug as she walked him to the door. "Don't forget," she said, "dinner tomorrow at six. We'll order out."

Olivia opened the door. She was surprised to find Brad standing on the other side, dressed in immaculate gray slacks, a pressed blue shirt, and Ray-Bans, looking like a tanned Italian billionaire and holding a cardboard drink carrier with two steaming coffees. The strong, rich aroma lit up all the caffeine-deprived centers of her brain. He handed her one and, without missing a beat, offered the other to her father. "Morning, Mr. Marks."

Olivia's father mumbled a non-enthusiastic "Morning, Bradley," and declined the coffee by holding up his hand.

"Does everyone around here rise before the chickens?" Olivia asked, making a feeble attempt to comb through her bed head with her fingers. She feigned indifference as Brad swung his shaded gaze slowly over her, but it was like the room temperature had just shot up twenty degrees. Like he'd drilled right through her rumpled exterior and was seeing her stark, buck naked—and liking it.

Heat blazed low and deep in her abdomen. Visuals of his strong, capable hands roving all over her body rolled unwanted through her brain. She was addicted to his particular type of pheromone crack, helpless in the face of it, regardless of how much she disliked other parts of him.

If only she was wearing makeup and a suit with heels, something dignified and professional. But she had the feeling that not even that protective armor would shield her from the sensual force that was Brad, leaving her as flustered as the girl she had been at eighteen.

Wait a minute. Why was he suddenly here with coffee, sucking up to her father? He'd certainly changed his tune from yesterday. It was time to act less like a nervous teenager and more like the guarded businesswoman she was.

Frank Marks eyed Brad warily as he navigated the steps down from the wooden deck. He'd always been leery of Brad. Halfway down the stairs he turned. "How's the construction coming on the restaurant?"

"We've managed to stay open through the chaos, but the grand opening celebration's in two weeks," Brad said. "And thanks for recommending Paul Dunn. The other electrician just wasn't working out." Brad's tone was nothing but friendly, compared to the edge in her father's voice.

"You're welcome. Think I will take one of those coffees after all." Olivia's father lifted the coffee from the carrier then waved a cursory good-bye as he climbed into his old white van with the ladder on top and *Mirror Lake Hardware* painted in navy letters on the side. As the van disappeared down the street, Olivia turned to Brad, who grinned widely.

"Look, I'm not sure why you're here, but I—"

Brad threw his hands up in surrender. "Hey, I come bearing coffee. And I came to apologize for being so . . ."

"Judgmental?"

He exhaled. "I was going to say unneighborly, but yes. Judgmental. I'm sorry."

His quirked-up smile looked sexy, not sorry.

"Then what's so funny?" she asked.

He shook his head. "I just find it hard to believe your father still wants to kill me after all these years."

"He senses what you did to me way back then."

"Take you to prom?" Brad asked innocently.

Olivia's cheeks flushed. "As I recall, we did a little bit more than just go to prom together." They stood in the doorway. She was blocking

Brad's way into the house and wasn't sure if she should move. The conversation seemed headed into dangerous territory.

He stepped closer. She could smell the light scent of his cologne—tasteful and expensive—and the lingering scent of menthol shaving cream. He loomed tall, his elegantly creased dress shirt fitting over his broad shoulders like a second skin. Sexy, successful, confident. More crack. "Let's see, I believe you're right." He pretended to rub his chin thoughtfully. "We also attended the senior picnic and canoe trip. The canoe trip was especially fun."

"We got lost and ended up alone in the rapids."

"See what I mean? Once we navigated the rapids, it was just me, you, and that canoe. *Especially* fun." Brad waggled his eyebrows.

"As I recall, riding the rapids wasn't the biggest thrill that day," she mumbled. Joking with him was irresistible, just like old times, but as soon as the words were out, she wished she could take them back. The images they conjured were too flirtatious. And too vivid.

"No, sweetness, it wasn't." Brad took off his sunglasses and trained those cool green eyes on her. His expression was unreadable but it unnerved her, sent tiny prickles of awareness pinging everywhere.

His old pet name renewed her blush. Or maybe it was from remembering how they'd beached that old canoe deep in some low-hanging tree branches and made desperate, sweet love for hours that sunny, steamy May afternoon. "Don't—call me that."

The past was too close, pushing on her, awakening old memories best forgotten. She had big problems to focus on and he was distracting her from them. They'd both moved on, for the better, of course.

"Thanks for the coffee," Olivia said, steering the conversation into safe territory. After all, he'd given up his for her dad. "How about we split this one?" She walked into the kitchen, happy to be on the move, and set the cup on the island. Brad trailed too close, right behind her.

As she searched the cabinets for a mug, he pulled off the lid and sipped, then handed it to her, like they were sharing a Coke in the old days. A simple, impulsive gesture, but it seemed too intimate. She turned, leaving the cupboard doors ajar, and took a sip. Strong, aromatic, rich. Within seconds, the caffeine fired up her sleepy neurons and set her heart racing. Or was that from Brad's nearness?

"Bet you won't find any junk food in there," Brad tipped his chin toward the open cabinets, "unless Kevin managed to hide a stash somewhere."

Olivia smiled. Trish had religiously followed an all-organic, no-caffeine diet all through her pregnancy. Her sister had always thrown herself into anything she did one hundred percent. Both of them possessed the same drive, just aimed it in completely different directions.

She was suddenly grateful Brad was here, joking and flirting. Keeping at bay the dark void that threatened to pull her in around every corner.

"It must be hard to stay here," Brad said, looking around the kitchen as if he'd sensed her fear and dread. The mail pile with catalogs to recycle and bills someone else would have to pay. A package wrapped with paper from a brown grocery bag, a birthday gift for a cousin that never made it to the post office. A pair of Kevin's flip-flops tossed off by the door.

And worst, the photos. Trish was obsessed with them. She took them, copied them, printed them, scrapbooked them, and hung them everywhere. Olivia could not glance in any direction without being inundated by happy, wonderful, heartbreaking moments.

Brad walked over to a bookshelf in the family room and picked up a framed picture. It was taken at the hospital, just after Annabelle was born. It was the typical pose of Trish in the hospital bed, Kevin's arm around her, the baby pink and new with a cap on her head and bundled in a white flannel hospital blanket. The expressions on the new parents' faces were jubilant, relieved, exhausted. They were both grinning from ear to ear.

"Who called you?" Brad asked.

Olivia must've looked puzzled, because he added, "You know. The night she was born. I just wondered which of us knew first."

So he still had his competitive streak. "Trish called me from home at dinnertime, before she went in. She was painting the hallway gray when her water broke."

"She wanted to finish before they went to the hospital," Brad said.

"Kevin was so upset. He couldn't understand why she was doing that. 'It didn't need painting' he said, 'and what was wrong with beige, anyway?' Being a lawyer, he always made a practical argument."

Olivia took a seat on the brown sofa, chuckling a little. "She wanted to throw laundry in, too. He'd almost had to force her into the car. That was just like her. She wanted everything to be neat and tidy when she came back with the baby. Poor Kevin had to finish painting the hallway on, like, an hour of sleep."

Brad replaced the frame. "I went to the hospital right after work. Annabelle wasn't born until midnight."

"I was in Chicago on business. I caught the first flight back but didn't get in till the next morning. I missed everything." She went quiet. "I let my sister down." When you were part of two sisters raised without a mother, that was a big deal. She would always feel guilty she'd missed the most important experience of her sister's life.

Brad looked surprised. "Don't say that. You did your best."

She shrugged, not believing him. "It was an extra trip. I could've said no."

"Trish wasn't due for two weeks. You couldn't have known." A sudden grin lit his face. "Besides, Trish FaceTimed you before they even let me in to see the baby. So looks like you win after all. You saw Annabelle first."

Except no one really won. Because here they were, in an empty house surrounded by memories.

Olivia was getting choked up so she walked back to the kitchen. For a minute the house was silent except for the soft static of the baby monitor.

Outside, birds created a morning riot and sunlight glittered on the shimmering dew. The tiny backyard surrounded by a rim of old trees created a brilliant explosion of green outside the door and a warm, fresh breeze blew in through the open window. A different world from New York. The geraniums planted in antique gold-rimmed barrels on the porch looked wilted, and Olivia made a mental note to water them. God knew she'd killed any living plant she'd ever laid hands on, but caring for the flowers Trish had so lovingly planted seemed elemental and urgent. Like keeping them alive kept part of her sister alive.

"How'd she do last night?" Brad leaned casually against the kitchen counter, tipping his head in the direction of the baby's room. His body was big and broad and lean, too big for the tiny kitchen, too big in her thoughts. She should have never let him in the house.

"Compared to what happened in Gertie's, much better," Olivia said, knowing that a good night for a one-month-old was a very relative term. "Chalk it up to exhaustion after all that crying."

His gaze strayed lazily over her again. "And how'd *you* do?"

"I . . . survived." She wondered what he thought of her messy hair, lack of makeup, her old T-shirt and cutoff sweats. While he wore billionaire businessman chic and looked tastier than that cinnamon roll she'd just scarfed down.

But she was not trying to impress him and she might as well be honest. "Look, about yesterday. I'm here to make a plan, to do what my sister asked of me. But I honestly don't know a thing about babies."

Brad's gaze wandered over the mile-high stack of baby care books piled on the kitchen table. Why was it so important that he see how hard she was trying? Even if she was the last person in the world Trish should have picked to be Annabelle's mom?

"Are you saying you might not keep her?" He sounded hopeful.

"No, I-I just want to learn all I can and do what's best for Annabelle." *Whatever that is.* "It's a little overwhelming."

She'd expected an argument, but instead Brad flashed a smile. Tiny lines she'd never noticed before crinkled at the corners of his eyes. They lent him an air of maturity that was unbelievably sexy. As if anything about him *wasn't*. He reached over and smoothed the unruly hair down on the top of her head.

Olivia cleared her throat and backed up a step. "That bad, huh?"

Brad shook his head. "I was just thinking you look like you're eighteen again. No makeup, your hair wild like that." She stared at him, watched emotion darken his eyes, and she could not look away. If she were less experienced, she'd think it was the pull of old memories, but Olivia was old enough to know pure, raw desire when she saw it.

Brad bent his head, his gaze locking on her lips. Her breath caught and for a moment she thought he was about to kiss her. She fought the compulsion to drag her fingers through his thick hair, press herself against his big strong body, use him as a comfort from all the confusion that had tipped her world. But that would be unbelievably wrong.

He raised his arm, as if to cup her cheek. Instinctively, she tilted up her head, ready to accept his kiss, but suddenly Brad thrust both his hands into his pants pockets. An awkward silence hung between them.

Olivia stepped far back, chiding herself. What was wrong with her? Drooling after a long-lost memory when a tiny baby who needed everything and had lost her whole world slept innocently one room away?

Brad pulled out a note from his pants pocket and cleared his throat. "I almost forgot. My grandma Effie gave me this to give you."

He handed over a small square of paper that was folded in fours. Glad for the distraction, Olivia opened it carefully and read the caption out loud. "Baby Care Classes—Mirror Lake Community Center. Starting tonight."

"Effie thought you might be interested. She used to teach them for years until she retired from nursing."

Hmmm. Baby care class. This could be just what she needed to give herself the skills she lacked.

She skimmed down the flyer. "They're for . . . couples. It says to take a spouse, significant other, parent, or friend." Great. Alex and Meg had a business meeting tonight. Her father would rather suffer through a bout of shingles than be trapped for an hour in a roomful of pregnant women. And she certainly didn't have a mother who could step in to help.

Going alone would be awkward. It would evoke pitying stares and solemn head shakes. But she needed the info. Bad.

"I'm not working tonight," Brad said. "I could go with you."

Sympathy lit his eyes, and that startled her. Weakened her. Oh, how he could still get to her, especially now, when she felt something she rarely ever felt in her professional life—vulnerable. On the edge of despair. Desperate for someone to hold her hand on this frightening journey.

"I couldn't ask that of you," she said guardedly. That would be uncomfortable. Tense. Awkward. *Wrong.* She would do it on her own as she had faced so many other challenges.

"Well, I am her uncle," Brad continued. "You'd have some company. Maybe you should accept help once in a while instead of going this alone."

She met his gaze. Brad still had that cool confidence, that easy, relaxed manner he'd always possessed. Olivia couldn't help being drawn in by those brilliant eyes, green as new leaves, unfathomable as the ocean.

"How about I pick you up at six?" he asked.

"Okay. It's a date." The answer poured from her mouth before she could stop it and she cringed at her weakness. *It's a date?* Where had that come from? From the bowels of her weak, weak resolve, that was where.

On cue, like the every-Wednesday-at-noon test of the community tornado siren that warned of disaster, Annabelle's sudden cry through the baby monitor rent the air between them. Olivia stepped back at once, snapping out of her Brad-induced trance.

As she rushed down the hallway to get the baby, Olivia groaned. Her mouth had clearly disconnected from her brain. Brad had sensed a weakness and he'd barged right in to prey upon it with his kind concern and his smoking hot body. And she'd fallen for it—her knees were shaking and her hands trembling, just like she was that naïve young girl who thought Brad Rushford held the world in his hands.

How could she suddenly trust him, when yesterday he'd been so angry and upset she'd gotten Annabelle? What on earth had changed, except for a few pheromones in the air that had clearly sucked away all her good sense? She'd fallen back so easily into bad habits. Trusting him when there were red flags everywhere warning her not to put her feet in that ocean.

Life was complicated enough. She could not allow him to complicate it further. She turned around and called his name. He halted at the door with a questioning look.

"I-I'm sorry, but I think it's best if I go alone. We're not a couple and I-I just wouldn't feel comfortable." She hesitated before adding, "Thanks anyway, though."

Brad's brows rose in a question, and he opened his mouth to speak. Instead he nodded his head and tossed her a polite smile. "Okay, Liv. See you around."

Once he'd left out the kitchen door, Olivia slapped a hand to her forehead. She'd handled that badly. But she'd done the right thing.

Brad Rushford hadn't lost his old talent to slip under her skin, reduce her to a puddle of melted syrup. And if she wasn't careful, he'd slip under her panties, too, and that would be a disaster.

He'd certainly changed his tone from yesterday. Apologizing, bringing coffee, *flirting*. It wasn't like him to suddenly do a complete one-eighty on his feelings. She didn't know what he was up to, but she was going to find out.

CHAPTER 4

"If I ran my business like this, I'd have no customers," Brad mumbled as he tapped the hand bell on top of a glass-cased counter at Bridal Aisle, which was filled with girly satin purses, earrings, and beaded shoes.

"Alex! Where the hell are you?" He looked warily around the destination shop his sister-in-law ran with her friend Meg Halloran. The rainbows of fancy dresses, the waif-like manikins with unnaturally skinny waists, and a table piled with bridal magazines made him realize he was in foreign territory, one he didn't want a passport for.

He was in a mood. Was having trouble concentrating at work, so he'd run over here on a quick errand to clear his head. It was a big mistake to have shown up with coffee this morning for his hot, sexy neighbor. He'd wanted to be friendly, cordial. How else could he convince her to do the right thing by Annabelle? Or find a weak spot he could infiltrate and seize the opportunity to find a better home for his niece?

He'd gone over there with the specific intention of getting on her good side. Catching more bees with honey and all that. But the baby class had unexpectedly created an opportunity he simply couldn't miss out on. She needed to see firsthand how much time and effort it took to raise a child. How much knowledge she lacked. That would be Step One to make her realize she was not the right person to be Annabelle's mother.

But he'd ended up being sucked in by her feminine force field, the exact same one that had crushed him when he was eighteen.

Seeing her all tousled made him think of ways to keep her up all night that had nothing to do with crying infants. Their back-and-forth banter kept him on his toes. And there was something about her . . . a steely determination in the face of fear that made every cell in his body want to help her in any way possible instead of to undermine her. Even though she didn't need it and would balk at the very suggestion of his aiding her in any way.

There he went again. Brad knew every single success he'd earned was due to a laser-like focus on his goals. He was not about to let Olivia's tight little ass or her melty cocoa eyes make him lose sight of his goal. *Annabelle's future.*

He'd do anything to secure that, including use Olivia's insecurities to his advantage. He had so little time, and so few tools at his disposal. There had to be a way to appeal to her intelligence, her sense of logic, to make her see the truth.

A pink curtain parted between the shop and the back room, and a pretty woman in a gray suit, hair piled up business-like on her head, approached the counter.

"Quit your fussing, Bradley, we're not even open yet." Alex glanced at his hands. "Oh, you brought the doll. Thank goodness." Her polished demeanor cracked with relief.

Brad waggled the floppy doll he carried. "Found it wedged between the wall and my couch. I have no idea how it got there."

"Sure you don't. You'd never roughhouse with my kids, would you?"

Brad pointed innocently to himself. "*Moi?* Never!"

She plucked the doll away. "We spent an hour last night looking for this."

"A whole hour? Isn't that a bit extreme?"

She rolled her eyes. "I can't wait till you have kids of your own so I can remind you that you actually said that."

A petite woman with long straight hair the color of black coffee waved at them from across the store. He hadn't seen her amid the racks of foofy dresses. She bounced a baby on her shoulder while humming a current pop song, her flowery peasant skirt swaying around her calves as she half walked, half danced through the aisles.

"Meg," Alex called out, leaning over the counter, "I'm pretty sure Olivia said she was only going to expose Annabelle to classical music. Somehow, I don't think Katy Perry qualifies."

Annabelle? Brad did a double take as Meg approached with the pink-clad infant. He was officially outnumbered by a feminine factor of three. At least sweet, ruffly Meg wouldn't hassle him whereas Alex, cashing in on the privilege of being his sister-in-law, would take free aim. With grenades.

Big blue eyes blinked up at him. He cupped Annabelle's head in one hand, her soft blonde baby fuzz tickling his skin. He was struck, as always, by her tininess. "Hey there, sugar. You're looking pretty today."

Annabelle didn't quite smile, but she kicked her legs, and Brad felt something in her steady, calm gaze that shot straight to his heart. *Recognition.* She knew who he was and was happy to see him. He *felt* it. A feeling of pleasure and pride ripped through him that renewed his determination to champion her at any cost.

Meg gathered her hair away from the baby's fists and draped it over her empty shoulder. "Oh, Annabelle's got to learn to have rhythm. She needs pop music for that, don't you, sweetie?"

Alex shook her head. "Meg, for as much as you love music, it's amazing you don't dance."

A blush worked its way into Meg's cheeks. She wasn't as shy as she'd been in high school, but still hated to be put on the spot. "Not in public, anyway. I never grew up with it. But that doesn't mean I don't feel the thrill of the music just the same."

Had Olivia dropped Annabelle off with her two best friends? Brad scanned the store again. He really didn't want to run into her, especially after she'd specifically *un*invited him to baby class.

"She's in the bathroom, taking a migraine pill." Meg was clearly onto him. "The past week's been a little rough."

Tell me about it. "Anything I can do?" he asked, knowing these two women had it covered. A quick glance at his phone told him he had to get back to work.

"Actually, yes." Meg handed Annabelle to him faster than a foul ball speeding down the third baseline to an unsuspecting fan in the stands. "Mrs. Kline and Priscilla are going to be here any minute and we've got to set up."

Brad readjusted the warm, sweet-smelling bundle. All of them had gone to school with Priscilla Kline, the mayor's daughter. Her wedding promised to be the Mirror Lake event of the century. If the minions survived the preparations.

Alex pointed to the back. "Olivia said something about Annabelle needing a bottle. Maybe you can help out for a few minutes?"

Brad really had to go. He had a conference call in fifteen minutes and his seafood supplier was bringing in the daily shipment that he always inspected personally. "Well, I—"

"Olivia's so sick, she just needs some time for the medicine to kick in before she can function again," Meg said solemnly.

He suspected a setup from the Two Musketeers, who'd reconnoitered similar missions in the past. Just then, the bell over the door tinkled and a gaggle of women entered, talking boisterously amongst themselves.

He had no desire to run into Priscilla, who'd had a larger-than-life crush on him a few years ago.

Besides, Olivia's guard would be down. Maybe he could use that to get her to see the error of her ways. Just then, Annabelle stared at him with her stellar baby blues and curled her tiny finger possessively around his pinky.

He always was a sucker for a pretty woman. "Where is she?" he said on a sigh.

Through the curtain, the large storeroom was dim. He spotted Olivia half sitting, half lying, her back to him, on an old velvet-cushioned settee.

"Alex, is that you?" Olivia called. "I'm about to hurl my breakfast all over your antique couch because I can't open this damn pill."

Brad bit back a grin. "Pass it over," he said, coming to stand next to her.

Startled, she looked up, her big brown eyes rounding even larger. She covered her forehead with her arm and slumped down further onto the couch. "Not *you* again. Please God, anyone but you."

"It's me, all right." He took a small foil packet from her and ripped it open with his teeth. "You look pretty stressed. That's not even all of it. All that gray, pasty skin, bags under your eyes . . ."

She didn't really look like hell. Okay, maybe a little. Mostly she looked exhausted, and he almost felt guilty for tormenting her.

There was a blotch of formula on the shoulder of her wrinkly white T-shirt and a threadbare spot on the thigh of her old jean shorts with white threads hanging down. She shouldn't have been sexy. But she was, dammit, even sick and pissed off.

Her toned legs stretched out for miles. He wanted to run his hands all over their smooth softness. Her hair was splayed out and wild around her head, begging for him to plow through its rich thickness. There was something about her reclining on that couch, exhausted, unguarded, yet wary, that overwhelmed him with the need to help her. Protect her. Jump her bones.

The jumble of conflicting feelings tormented him. What was *wrong* with him? He'd have to get his pleasure by tormenting the hell out of her instead.

She snatched at the pill but he held it just out of reach.

Outrage washed across her face in bright hues of red. He almost smiled at how much he was still able to agitate her. "Get these headaches often?"

"No, it's just the lack of sleep, the stress." She almost grabbed it that time, but he was still on his game.

"And you aren't even working now. Just wait till you've got to be up all night with a baby then have to negotiate your six-figure deals the next day."

"Hand me my medicine or I swear to God you'll die in your sleep tonight."

"Coming, coming." He handed her the packet and a paper cone of cold water from the corner water cooler. "Plus you're a perfectionist who'll demand a lot of yourself . . . and Annabelle."

Olivia's response was to shoot him a death glare over the top of the paper cup.

"Alex said Annabelle needed a bottle. I'd be happy to feed her." The baby was still in his arms, sucking quietly on her fingers. She was a warm little football-sized bundle, compact and cute as a Christmas puppy. He loved his niece and nephews, but this little thing—well, he'd never had such a strong urge to safeguard anyone from harm.

Maybe it was the baby's blissful unawareness that the entire trajectory of her life had been altered in a single moment. It was too terrible a blow, and he wanted to do everything in his power to shelter her from any others.

Brad rummaged through the diaper bag. "You know what happens to kids raised by perfectionist mothers."

Olivia was lying almost flat on the settee, elbow crooked over her forehead. She groaned softly, from aggravation or pain, he wasn't sure. "Please, please go away."

"Right after this story. You know Sally Hopkins, don't you? Drove her daughter up to Julliard to sing for an admission tryout and the poor girl was so stressed, not one sound came out. Like she was mute or something."

Olivia looked at him like he was a pure, raving lunatic.

"Never did sing in public again. Want to know what she's doing now?"

"No, but I have a feeling you're going to tell me anyway."

"She heads up the late show at the truckers' lounge out on route fifty-four. Heard she does a hell of a rendition of 'You Light Up My Life.'"

"You can totally leave now."

"Isn't there a bottle in here somewhere?"

"Yes, and I can handle it. I really don't need your help."

"As I recall, I think you said that before, the other day in Gertie's, and we all know how that turned out." He found a full bottle, and took it to the small employee break area where he ran it under some warm water. Then he rummaged through the old corner fridge. "Here you go." He placed a towel with ice wrapped inside not un-gently over her forehead.

"You're like the man who rocks the cradle while he pinches the baby. You pretend you're being helpful, but the whole time, you're subverting me."

He bit back a grin. "Honey, I'd love to subvert you, but I don't have time now. I've got to get back to work."

She sat up, wincing and grabbing her head. Then squinted at him like the dim light in the room was the Red Sox stadium floodlights. "I'm good now. Hand her over."

He shook his head and pushed her firmly back onto the settee. "So prideful. You'd still rather cut your right arm off than ask for help."

"Since I'm left-handed, that might not be such a big deal." He moved the ice bag to better cover her forehead and this time she didn't fight him. "And *you* still have that same overdeveloped sense of responsibility."

"Other parts of me are overdeveloped, too."

"When I saw them last, they weren't that developed."

"As I recall, the only complaints that ever passed your lips about my size were that you were afraid you couldn't take it all."

41

"You must be mistaking your ego for your penis."

He laughed. Couldn't help himself. Some perverse part of him loved her wit, her humor, her sass *way* too much.

Brad stole a glance as Olivia leaned her head against the cushion. He was glad her eyes were closed, because he couldn't take his off her. Dark, arched brows, long lashes, a beautiful oval face. He could do wicked things with those full pink lips, taste them and lick them and nip them and thrust his tongue deep until she whimpered low in her throat. Rove his hands over her fine breasts and her flat, taut stomach until they were both begging for more.

A volley of memories shot at him right and left, pummeling him with all the times they'd been desperate for each other, out of control and frantic with need.

He distracted himself by gazing over at the platform where all the brides stood to look at themselves in their dresses. "And then there's that dais with the three-way mirrors."

Olivia cracked open an eye. "What about it?" she asked cautiously.

"Don't tell me you don't remember that time you were working late and we came back here and turned on those runway lights and . . ."

"Okay, okay."

"Remember when Alex's aunt came back to investigate the noise?" Brad asked. "We hid in that tiny closet over there."

They'd been buck naked, he failed to mention out loud. He still remembered the feel of her silky warm skin, smooth and soft and naked under his roving teenage hands.

God, that was the best sex of his pathetic, hardworking teenage life. Weird thing was, maybe it was the best sex ever. And that was just plain scary.

Olivia cleared her throat. "This place still smells the same as ever."

"Rotty hundred-year-old wood and this morning's burnt coffee. What's not to love?"

"I was thinking more in terms of lilac and rose sachets. They were stored in that closet with us, remember? You know, for the brides."

Brad couldn't tell one flower from another if it came down to his life, but as far as smells went, the smell of rain always reminded him of her. When they were seventeen, he'd walked her home from his soccer game and they'd gotten stuck in a downpour. They'd run into the gazebo in the middle of the town square to wait it out. One minute they were running and laughing and out of breath, and the next he was just staring at her, mesmerized by the raindrops coating her long lashes, her smooth, soft skin, and the sudden serious look in her eyes. Their gazes locked, their smiles faded, and he'd kissed her. The perfect beauty of that moment had stayed with him all this time.

Olivia looked over at the runway, as if she was eager to change the subject. "This is a magical place. Generations of brides have come through here to start their happily-ever-afters."

He snorted, mostly to try and push away the nostalgia that had socked him so hard in the gut. "I'm sure Alex and Meg buy into all that baloney."

Olivia frowned. "Wow, who soured you on love?"

A loaded question, considering their past.

"I'm just being realistic. Love isn't a fairy tale. It leads to a lifetime of responsibility—kids, a house, car payments, college expenses."

"I'm sure it was hard raising your siblings but you've done a great job. Aren't you proud?"

She had no idea how badly he'd messed that up. Especially his little sister Samantha, who rebelled every blessed chance she got. "Love is a luxury for teenagers who have time to be moony about it," Brad said. "For everyone else it leads to harsh realities."

"I don't care what you say. Love is magical. The feeling when it's right is the best, most perfect feeling in the world, and you have no choice but do everything in your power to make it work."

Brad hadn't understood that at nineteen. He'd been too overwhelmed by work, by the feeling that his own future was on hold for his family. What could he have offered her, when her life was beginning to soar and his was grounded by financial and family burdens and cares? He would only have dragged her down.

What they had way back then had been special, but they'd been kids. He wondered what she thought about it. But he couldn't go there—it was too personal, too deep.

Or maybe it was just too damn scary.

He adjusted the nearly empty bottle so Annabelle didn't swallow air. "Frankly, I'm surprised you think that way after your mom took off."

He had little recollection of Olivia's mother. But his grandmother had told him she'd been an archaeologist who'd felt suffocated in Mirror Lake. One day she left for a dig in Rome, met a guy there, and never came back for as much as a stitch of clothing or a single possession.

And definitely not for her two little girls.

"Maybe that made me believe in it even more," Olivia said. "I constantly dreamed of what life would be like if she suddenly decided she couldn't live without us, if she came back."

She kicked off her shoes and sighed. A simple movement, but it fascinated him, like so much else about her. Much to his chagrin.

"The fairy tale never lasts. Like what we had in high school." He shouldn't have brought it up. But part of him needed to know, did she feel like he had back then? Or had he just embellished it for all these years?

Olivia removed the ice pack and sat up a little. Their gazes locked. Bridal Aisle fell away. Had any woman—and there'd been plenty—ever possessed the ability to stop him dead in his shoes like she did, with that clear, honest gaze that drilled right through all his bullshit with a single glance?

"That was first love," she finally said, her voice low and quiet.

"What's your verdict on that?"

She shrugged. "It was wonderful, intense, scary, and . . . I was completely swept off my feet."

Loving her had been a wild, uncontrolled, crazy ride. He'd put his whole heart out there, gave her everything he had. It had been an impossible love from the start, between a brainy girl who was going places and a hack like him, barely getting by in school. But somehow it was magic.

When he'd visited her that first fall at NYU, he'd been as out of place as a Picasso in an antique shop. By Christmas, they'd become more uncomfortable around one another. She talked of studying abroad and internships in the City with publishing companies. He hadn't even considered college a possibility with his family's financial status teetering as precariously as a high wire in a big wind.

That Christmas, she'd come home. It was snowing, and they'd gone for a walk in the town square. The Christmas tree that she'd always loved was decorated and lit, right next to the big white gazebo where bands played and kids caroled. Where he'd first kissed her when they were seventeen.

But that year, all she talked about was the millions of lights on the Rockefeller Center tree, how huge it was, how it was the greatest tree she'd ever seen. That—yes, that simple comment—was the beginning of the end.

Her dreams were as big as that Rockefeller tree. Too big for him. He was like that puny tree—simple, unsophisticated, not glitzy. His love would drag her back here and crush her dreams and he couldn't abide that. He'd had no choice but to let her go.

Lots of high school lovers break up. It's a rite of passage for many. People realize they've grown apart and move on, and soon the old love is forgotten. He'd told himself that for many years, yet it sometimes seemed that his feelings for Olivia were like gum on your shoe—persistent, still there after you've scraped it off a zillion times.

Olivia's voice brought him back to the present. He was glad to see she'd changed the subject. "Look," she said. "I know I didn't have the best example in my life to show me how to be a mother. But you learned to be a father to your siblings and I can learn how to take care of Annabelle, too. Even if it is the scariest thing I've ever done."

Her determination in the face of her fear got to him. His impulse was to comfort, but he bit back the words. Ones that would tell her she was doing her best and it would all work out, regardless of the scars her mother had left behind.

"I know you'll do the right thing for Annabelle." Weak, but what could he say? In Brad's experience, people didn't change. He'd almost forgotten that Olivia would always be a hard-driving, high-achieving woman. And Annabelle would suffer for it.

From the diaper bag, Olivia's cell phone rang. Brad picked it up and read the caller name. "It says *Sylvia*," he said.

"My boss. I have enough headaches now." She hand signaled to him to put the phone back. "I'll talk to her later."

"How is your job? You edit self-help books?"

"Relationships, self-esteem, work-life balance, overcoming adversity, getting organized." She smiled. "I love it."

"Why?" She'd always read a lot as a teenager, but he'd usually seen her with romance novels.

"When you have as messed up a childhood as I had, self-help books are tantalizing. They teach you that there are a whole lot of other people just as screwed up as you are. And that gives hope."

Interesting. "Which one's your favorite?"

"Hard to say. *Putting Karma Back into the Kama Sutra* was a blockbuster. Huge."

"*You* edited that?"

She laughed, a deep, belly laugh with a little snort she couldn't control. He hadn't heard her laugh like that in years. "I'm teasing,

Brad. Just teasing. I just wanted to prove you're not beyond looking at self-help books, either."

"Honey, I'm never ashamed to be an innovator. Not that my skills need improvement, mind you. But I'm always open to new ideas. Especially *that* kind, if you know what I mean." He waggled his brows for emphasis.

He'd made her blush. Good, because she deserved a little payback. He'd forgotten how funny she could be. Together, they could joke and tease and play off one another like the old days. And that was a very scary thought.

Meg popped her head around the door. "They're gone. Oh, can I hold her?"

"She . . . needs to be burped, and I've got to get back to work." Brad handed Meg the baby, suddenly desperate for some fresh air.

"Oh, I love burping babies," Meg said as she hoisted Annabelle over her shoulder and rubbed her back.

Alex handed Olivia a cold can of diet soda. "Here, honey, thought this might hit the spot."

"Thank you all for helping me," Olivia said. She turned to Brad. "And you for tormenting me."

"Always a pleasure." He made certain to sweep his gaze slowly up and down her body, lingering at all the right places just to piss her off.

And he was pleased to see another bright scarlet flush spread up her face.

As Brad walked out, he caught a whiff of lavender and the faint, sweet smell of roses. All that sappy talk must have gotten to him. He breathed in a big lungful of lake air to clear his head.

Olivia was clearly a woman struggling to come to terms with events that had pitched her whole world into a careening tilt. But he preferred the Evil Editor version. Less complicated, less hard on his libido. Not to mention his heart.

The way he saw it, he had a few choices. He could get her into bed and do certain things that would drain the fight right out of any normal woman and reduce her to a whimpering, sated heap of jelly. The sexual currents certainly still buzzed strong between them.

But knowing all the kick and fight in Olivia, she'd brawl with him to her last gasp.

No, with a sassy chick like her, he'd have to approach it more cerebrally. She'd admitted her soft spot, the one part that wasn't protected by that sarcastic coat of armor. So he'd use it, all right—and find a way to get her to realize on her own she wasn't the right person to raise Annabelle. He might have helped with her headache, but he was not going to help her become Annabelle's mom.

CHAPTER 5

Later that afternoon, migraine tamed, Olivia stepped into the sunny lobby of Mirror Lake Assisted Living, expecting to find Brad's grandmother patiently waiting on one of the sprawling, comfy couches in the theater-style reception area. What she hadn't expected was to see Brad's image, supersized, on the giant television screen.

She set down Annabelle's baby carrier to stare. The bright green eyes that haunted most of her waking moments crinkled as his lips curved into a smile. He full-out laughed, taking him from handsome to off-the-charts dangerous and shooting an electric frizzle clear down to her toes. Normal-size Brad was mesmerizing enough, but this was flat-out ridiculous.

The ring of Olivia's cell phone forced her attention away. The name *Sylvia* appeared on the screen. Her boss again.

"Ryan Connor's upset you're gone," Sylvia said.

Their biggest client. America's self-help guru, who was writing a sequel to his book on being assertive that was certain to be another blockbuster.

Olivia straightened one of Annabelle's socks, which were perpetually on the verge of falling off. "I e-mailed him I'd be back in two weeks. Helen can handle things until then."

"He's not used to working with Helen. He wants you. And you know how obsessive he is. He's insisting on face-to-face meetings."

"Tell Helen to forward me any e-mails she's concerned about. And tell Ryan I'll meet with him all he wants when I get back. There will still be plenty of time to go through the whole book again."

"And how're the relationship book edits coming? I know you're dealing with some tough shit but I was wondering if you'd had a chance to get to any of that?"

Ah, Sylvia. Always such a soft heart.

The answer to her question was, yes, Olivia had. For the ten free minutes she'd had last night before she passed out at the kitchen table. At midnight, she awakened to Annabelle's cries, only to find her cheek had been pressed to the keyboard and the screen was full of hundreds of *ZZZZZs.*

"I'm working on it," Olivia said. "I promise to deliver everything by deadline. You know I always do."

"You're a talented editor and a hard worker. But Ryan Connor is a major, major player and I simply can't risk his unhappiness."

"I've never let you down before, Sylvia. I won't now."

Olivia rubbed the right side of her forehead. Was that her migraine returning? She had to have a real discussion with her boss. One that involved the issue of cutting back her hours, because how else could she make this work? But instinct told her now was not the time.

She finished the call and slipped her phone back into her purse just as a snow-white cap of hair appeared over the back of one of the reception area couches, followed by the bespectacled face of Brad's grandmother, who waved her over. "Olivia, there you are. Yoo-hoo, dear, come sit and get settled while the show is on commercial."

"Effie," Olivia said with relief, picking up Annabelle's carrier and walking over to hug the older woman. "What show?" She hadn't come here to watch TV, or be exposed to larger-than-life Brad. She needed to talk, to be the recipient of some of the wraparound comfort Effie had always supplied in times of distress. A little selfish maybe, but these were desperate times.

Effie sat down carefully and patted the couch cushion next to her. She wore a bright pink cardigan and spotless white tennis shoes, and smelled of old-fashioned drugstore fragrance . . . like Emeraude or Chantilly. Familiar and comforting.

"Bradley's being interviewed about that charity event he's hosting over Memorial Day weekend." Effie perused Annabelle, who sat quietly in her carrier, four fingers stuffed happily in her mouth. "My goodness, she's grown since last week. And she does look like Patricia!" Effie patted Olivia's hand. "I'm so glad you came, dear."

"I wanted to see you." Olivia looked into Effie's eyes, the same startling green as Brad's. Uncanny, how much that gaze was like her grandson's. Olivia quickly shifted her own gaze to the baby, who was dressed in a tiny sundress sprinkled with strawberries and bumblebees and a matching sun hat. Olivia squatted down next to her and ran a finger over her velvety cheek before undoing the straps of her carrier.

She wanted to tell Effie so many things. Things she couldn't share with her grieving father, but that she surely would have told her sister. Like how her heart squeezed when she thought of this baby, so alone. Except for her, the scary caretaker.

The last few hours had become a comedy of errors. She'd slept off her headache while the baby napped, but then it had taken another hour between soothing, feeding, and changing before she finally got herself decently dressed. Another hour before she could put on makeup—at least enough to camouflage the dark circles. She'd finally dressed Annabelle and set out again.

"Oh, it's starting." Effie clasped her hands together in excitement then gestured to the remote. "Turn it up, would you, honey?"

Olivia placed Annabelle on Effie's lap and sat.

Olivia cranked the volume and stared at Brad's chiseled body, secretly enjoying the opportunity to stare that she wouldn't have in real life. He reclined gracefully at an outdoor table in a finely tailored suit, his shirt as white as his straight, beautiful teeth. The wind gently stirred the thick layers of his dark hair, the sun picking up its golden highlights. Olivia felt like she was watching a movie shot in the Riviera with a sexy male lead instead of a local news interview.

"That's Erika Peters, from Channel Five. She's working with Bradley on the Bachelors Who Cook event."

Next to him sat a sultry woman with glossy black hair and pouty lips who could have been the missing Kardashian sister with her defined cheekbones and sexy curves. She spoke into the camera. "I'm working *very* closely with successful entrepreneur Brad Rushford, who's kindly offered to host Bachelors Who Cook at his newly remodeled restaurant Reflections."

"Brad owns four other restaurants in the southeast area, including the new Vino in New London, which just got an excellent Zagat rating," Ms. Peters said. "What's next, Brad? We've heard rumors of a new restaurant in Philly or some even say Paris. Talk about a local boy making good."

"My restaurants are doing well," Brad said. "But I'm especially proud of the one here in Mirror Lake. If it helps bring people to town where they can discover everything we have to offer, all the better."

Effie beamed. "I'm so proud of him. He was fifteen when his parents passed, you know. And then I had that heart attack and couldn't work. And trying to feed and clothe and get five children through college on a nurse's salary—Lord, we've been through a lot. But I feel like he's my own child." She sat with her hand pressed over her heart, proudly beaming at the TV and holding Annabelle tightly.

As the camera panned around the restaurant, Brad explained the renovations. It looked like a pretty, open place, right on the water, and nothing like the crab shack of its previous incarnation. He used to dream about owning his own restaurant. How did he feel now that he'd become more successful than he ever imagined?

"Tell us what you love about your home town," Erika Peters said as she fingered his biceps, then made an "oooh" expression at the camera with her pretty, pouty mouth. She was perky and sexy, and *way* too familiar with Brad. Olivia cleared her throat of the thick, distasteful feeling caught there.

"Well, I like lots of things about Mirror Lake. I like the people—especially my grandma Effie, who's out there watching. Hey there, Effie, love you!" Brad, wearing a big grin, waved unabashedly at the camera.

"He always was a ham, wasn't he?" Effie mumbled, clearly pleased.

"Sure was." So clearly, Olivia remembered a younger version of that handsome face, showing off on her eighteenth birthday just for her. She could still see the pom-poms swaying on his sombrero as he sang "La Bamba" at her front door, accompanied by a Mariachi band comprised of their school marching band friends. Much to her father's chagrin.

And a more serious version, leaning against a big oak near the moonlit lake, shooting her a smile that sent tremors through her body and reduced her to a boneless pile of shivers. He'd cradled her face so gently in his big hands, his gaze bright and intense, his voice low and caressing. "There's no one else for me, Liv. No one." Then he'd kissed her, slow and gentle, till her toes curled and her knees buckled and every last thought in her head turned hazy and indistinct.

Dramatic and intense, or comedic and crazy. That was the Brad she once knew and loved.

For the millionth time, she tried to piece together exactly what had torn them apart. Brad had come to visit her, once, in the fall when she'd left for college. He hadn't even been able to stay an entire weekend. Maybe she'd been too exuberant about all the fun she'd been having. He hadn't liked her friends. Wasn't interested in hearing about her classes. Their differences had created a chasm that only seemed to widen with time.

It hadn't mattered to her that he wasn't in school. God knew he was working multiple jobs, struggling to keep his family afloat. He had more maturity and determination than so many of the boys she'd met in college.

But it had mattered to him. Brad had grown more sullen and distant, their fights more frequent. One evening at Christmastime, he'd sat with her on a bench on the town square and said it just wasn't working for him anymore.

She'd begged him not to break up with her. With a love as big as theirs, they could overcome anything, couldn't they? But it was too late. Their relationship train was pulling out of the station, and he'd refused to board. She'd stayed there alone, in the park at dusk on a snowy evening, watching the snow swirl around the lamplight, feeling the big, fat flakes land on her face and melt there with her tears, until she could no longer feel her fingers or toes.

And that was when she vowed never to come back to this small town. She'd make her future far away from all the heartbreak of a mother leaving and of the biggest love she'd ever known gone bad.

"Oh, listen," Effie said. "They're talking about the event. You know, I think that woman has a crush on Bradley."

"Whatever makes you think *that?*" Olivia crossed her one leg over another and bounced her foot up and down.

". . . and it's for a great cause, isn't it, Brad?" Erika scooted a little closer and nudged him with a bare shoulder, tapped his thigh with her hand. Olivia felt a pain in her own thigh. She glanced down to find her fists clenched, fingernails digging into her skin.

They're just playing up the Bachelor event. It's all about advertising and making Brad look appealing. Then why did the slow burn in her chest make her feel like mainlining Tums? And why did she nurse a deep desire to track Erika down and bind her up with microphone cord so she couldn't touch Brad?

"All the money's going to Mirror Lake Community Hospital," Brad said. "We're going to have live music and great food, and the bachelors are getting auctioned off after the cooking competition, so everyone should come on down to the waterfront."

"And how many bachelors will be showcasing their cooking talents?"

"We've got a dozen, all of us Mirror Lake businessmen and professionals."

"I'm excited to announce that you're one of the bachelors, Brad. So ladies, come prepared to bid. That's Memorial Day, at the waterfront, 6:00 p.m." She reached out and grasped Brad's jaw and shook it playfully. "You are so cute!" She let out a giggle. Brad raised a brow, but didn't move away. "Sorry," Erika said into the camera, "I just couldn't resist sampling the merchandise."

"Did she just *touch* him on the *face*?" Olivia's mouth dropped open. She snapped it shut before she realized she'd just said that out loud. Fortunately, Effie was too engrossed to hear.

Olivia rose from the couch and walked to a side table with an automatic beverage brewer where she busied herself with making tea, grateful for an excuse to collect her thoughts.

Seemed like everyone in Mirror Lake was smitten with Brad. Men liked him, women were crazy for him. And he was clearly very involved in the community. She scowled at his image, still grinning widely on the television. He certainly seemed to be enjoying promoting his event with Erika.

The reporter was outgoing, sexy, and flirty. She was probably fun-loving, too. Olivia could see the appeal, and the stark contrast to her own life. She tended to date men who were working their way up the professional ladder as she was, with little time for relaxation. Her relationships got sandwiched in between long work hours and high-pressure deadlines. She wondered for the thousandth time if putting her personal life on hold for so many years to achieve her goals had been the right thing to do.

She wished Effie weren't so into the show so they could have a real talk. Olivia placed the tea on the coffee table and sat down again.

"Effie, I—"

"One second, dear. Brad's talking to the mayor and the business council." Effie remained mesmerized. At last she glanced down at Annabelle, who had fallen asleep in her arms. "Oh, would you take the baby? I'm getting a crick in my elbow."

Olivia lifted Annabelle and set her gently in her car seat. At last the show went to break. Effie grabbed Olivia's hand, held it in both of her old, soft ones. "You'll have to forgive me for being so excited about this crazy bachelor event. If you two had stayed together, I wouldn't have to be so concerned about Brad meeting a nice woman and settling down."

"That was high school, Effie. We were just kids."

"Well, you're not children anymore, are you, and neither of you is married." She patted her hand and smiled a matchmaking grandma smile. "Oh, but things are so different now, aren't they?"

She said it facetiously, but they *were* different. In too many ways to count. Suddenly, the lump was back blocking her throat.

Effie squeezed Olivia's hands tightly. "Your whole life has changed faster than a gambler can bet away his fortune." Effie hadn't lost her talent to read her so well, even after all these years. "We're all feeling lost, after all that's happened. But look right there." She canted her head toward the baby. "At that little bundle of trouble sitting in that fancy baby contraption. Both her parents live on through her."

Olivia pulled a hand loose from Effie's grip and reached down to fiddle with the car seat straps. "Effie, I—" She wanted to say she just couldn't do it, couldn't be the mother Trish would have been, but she couldn't form the words.

Effie lovingly watched the sleeping baby. Annabelle's little hand was splayed across her cheek, her breathing low and regular. "You may not believe this now," she said softly, glancing up at Olivia, "but Trish and Kevin knew what they were doing when they named you this baby's guardian."

No, they didn't. Trish always thought the best of people. She was accepting whereas Olivia was eternally suspicious. That trait had gotten Trish taken advantage of frequently. Not to mention caused her to make a choice for Annabelle more based on emotion—or sisterly bonds or whatever—than logic. And somehow managed to convince Kevin of it, too.

In her experience, emotional decisions didn't move you up in the world. They got you demoted or fired. She'd seen it happen, and she was way too street-smart for that.

Olivia wondered again why they hadn't told her, asked her, explained exactly what the hell it was they were thinking? Surely they'd meant to. Kevin was a lawyer, for God's sake. All she knew was that the wills were dated the day before the baby's birth. Maybe in all the excitement, they'd simply forgotten.

Effie shook her head vehemently. "Not a mistake."

"I'm not sure I should keep her," Olivia blurted.

The theme music sounded again, but Effie fumbled on the remote for the mute button. She gave Olivia her full attention.

"I work all the time—twelve-hour days, mostly. Weekends, too. I can't keep those kinds of hours and raise a child. It would be . . . unfair."

Effie mulled that over. She took a while before she answered. "Goodness, Olivia, you always were so responsible and serious. It's what got you that big scholarship to begin with. Your head's going a mile a minute with all this worrying. Try turning the head off for a while and just be yourself. Then a decision will come."

Going from responsible and serious to carefree and living in the moment wasn't really going to happen with all the crushing decisions Olivia had to make. But as Annabelle slept and Effie told her stories of the other Rushford children and their goings-on, she found herself relaxing a little.

"Don't forget the big picnic this weekend," Effie said. "You will come, won't you?"

"Picnic?" Olivia's neck prickled with unease. Rushford picnics were legendary, and she was certain Brad never missed one.

Whether she liked it or not, Brad would always be in her life. That fate was sealed the day Trish married Kevin, and now Annabelle would ensure its continuance. She might as well get used to it.

Now Olivia felt the tug of an additional obligation. She was Annabelle's link to the Rushford family, responsible, for her sake, for maintaining and strengthening it. "Of course we'll be there."

She'd go to the picnic and catch up with the Rushford clan. She wouldn't avoid Brad. Seeing him as part of life in Mirror Lake would desensitize her to the explosive hormonal reaction that took control of her body every time she approached within ten feet of him—or a TV screen. Soon she'd come to realize Brad was just an old memory, best kept bundled and tied off like old love letters in the attic. He'd lose his appeal, just like day-old coffee.

Bitter, old, and best tossed for a fresh pot.

Besides, he was nowhere near ready to settle down. Watching him flirt with Erika proved that. And, she suddenly realized, what she wanted—what she *needed*, for Annabelle, was the possibility of a real family. Getting involved with him would only be asking for heartbreak.

She'd attend the picnic for Annabelle's sake, and Effie's. Not Brad's.

And she'd prove to herself she was over him once and for all.

CHAPTER 6

"Real or fake?"

Brad looked up from his laptop as he sat at a table on the newly built deck of Reflections. He'd been so immersed in number crunching that he barely noticed his brother Tom drop his large muscle-bound cop frame into the chair opposite him.

"It's made of some superstrong material that's fifty times more durable than wood and guaranteed to last forever," Brad answered.

"I'm not talking about flooring."

"Isn't that why you're here? To help me with the deck?"

"Yes, but you've been working way too hard if you have no clue what I'm talking about."

"So what the hell *are* you talking about?"

"Erika. Peters. *You know*." Tom gestured by placing his hands up to his chest in the universal boobs sign.

Around them, late afternoon sun glistened off waves that slapped against the sides of the deck. Seabirds dipped in and out of the deep blue water. It would have been a perfect, tranquil scene except for the pounding of hammers and the whir of a saw.

"Our first date is tonight," Brad said, trying to sound more enthused than he felt. Around them, workers milled about, carrying long planks. Two shuffled by, sharing the weight of an industrial-sized sink bowl. The smell of fresh cut wood carried on the slightly fishy-in-a-good-way breeze. Brad loved it—the smell of progress.

"Thought you'd be more excited. You've been talking about this date for weeks now. And I'm looking forward to hearing some details."

He had been excited. But now . . . not so much. Maybe he was getting too obsessed over this remodel. "I never tell you details. Alex would never forgive me."

"I'm a happily married man but I consider it my duty to know everything so I can counsel you. You know, so you can experience marital bliss one day, too."

"I don't need your counsel. I'm the big brother, remember?"

"And I'm the one married with three kids, four and under."

"You just want me to sympathize with your sex- and sleep-deprived state. How is everyone, by the way?"

"The kids miss not having Annabelle around, but I must admit we're getting a little more sleep."

Annabelle. Brad tapped his fingers on the table. "Actually, I wanted to ask you—"

One of the workers called out. "Hey, Brad, we're going to leave this pile of lumber out here for the night. That okay?"

Brad pointed to the far end of the new deck. "As long as it's stored in the new section. We aren't letting anyone eat there till the fencing's up."

Tom looked around. "The place is looking good, bro. Who'd have thought old Mr. Saunders's crab shack would turn into this?"

A feeling of pride bloomed in Brad's chest. The expansion doubled the seating capacity, and it was all directly on the lake. Boats could now pull up to the dock and anchor there. Reflections had become a destination restaurant and that was great for him and for his town.

His brother Kevin had conceived of the deck. He'd always had a great head for business, better than Brad did in some ways. "Make your restaurant the one everyone wants to come to," he'd said. "And make it accessible by water and land. People love to eat on the water." If only he could be here to see it now.

That same loss hit Brad, an empty void that snuck up on him no matter how busy he was. But a more urgent matter tugged on his mind. *Annabelle's future.* Tom and Alex were terrific parents. And they loved Annabelle. If they took her, she would grow up with other kids in a loving family. It was the perfect arrangement. He was pretty certain Tom would agree.

He was still baffled Trish and Kevin had named Olivia the baby's guardian. What were they thinking? Not that she wasn't loving or kindhearted, but her life was a roller coaster that never stopped.

Brad didn't take it personally they hadn't named him. He didn't think Kevin had held it against him that he was a tough older brother who demanded that all his siblings toe the line. Maybe Kevin knew in his heart what Brad feared the most—that he'd done a botch job, learning by the seat of his pants. He would never want to screw up another kid. The risks were way too high of that happening even under the best of circumstances. Yes, he was relieved it hadn't been him.

Now he just had to convince Tom that Annabelle belonged with them.

"You've worked hard for everything you got. We're proud of you." Tom patted his shoulder.

"Thanks." Brad always felt uncomfortable taking praise, but especially from his younger brother. He was usually the one to do the praising. Or the scolding. Or whatever it was his siblings needed. "We'll be ready for Bachelors Who Cook in two weeks. You and Alex are coming, right?"

"It's on the calendar."

"I wouldn't want to compete with something like an end-of-the-year preschool program."

"Well, Tommy does have a T-ball game tonight, so I'd like to get to laying that flooring for you."

Brad closed his laptop and shoved a stack of papers underneath so they wouldn't blow away. It was time for the truth. "I'm glad you came, but I want to talk to you about Annabelle."

"Is something wrong?"

He eyed his brother. He had to make him see. "No. Just that Olivia's got her hands more than full."

"She's been talking to Alex on the phone, getting advice. It's a big adjustment—for everybody."

Brad tapped a pencil against the table. He thought of Olivia, struggling and exhausted. That morning in the bridal shop, he'd let his guard down, but that would not happen again. It was the sex thing . . . if he'd been getting some, Olivia wouldn't get to him like she did. His date tonight with Erika should fix that problem for sure. It was time to be bold and focus on the best solution for everybody.

"Look, I've got nothing against Olivia, but Annabelle should stay here with us, in Mirror Lake, not be carted off to New York City."

"Whoa." Tom folded his arms and tipped back in his chair. "Do you know what you're saying? The will said Olivia gets her. That can't be changed."

"It can if Olivia agrees."

"Now you've just plain lost it."

"Olivia will never leave New York. She works all the time. Annabelle will be raised by a nanny. What kind of life is that for a kid?"

Tom squinted his eyes, and not because of the sun. "Exactly what are you proposing?"

"Olivia knows the right thing to do. She just may need a little . . . convincing." To be honest, Brad felt a little guilty for plotting against her. The feeling faded when he pictured Annabelle being raised as an only child far away from cousins who would toughen her up a little, provide companionship, and pull her out of the stark solitude of an only-child's life.

In his own life, having four younger siblings had been a burden in many ways. But losing both their parents so tragically had forged a bond of steel between them that would never be broken. It was the only thing that had gotten him through that terrible time. He knew beyond a doubt that any of his siblings would have his back at any time. And he wanted Annabelle to feel that. There was a special strength in forging family bonds when you don't have parents and he knew that firsthand.

Tom shook his head. "I understand how you'd want to keep Kevin's kid here. We'd all like to keep a piece of him here. But Olivia's making a big effort. Alex says she's going to drop her hours some. I mean, who are we to judge?"

"Yes, we can judge," Brad said defiantly. The pencil snapped in half. "We can tell Olivia as a family what we think is best. Like, a group recommendation."

Tom snorted. "You mean gang up on her? We've known Olivia a long time. I'm sure she'll do the best she can for Annabelle. Besides, even if Olivia did give up Annabelle, who would take her?"

Brad stared at his brother.

"Oh, no." Tom held out both hands in a *no way* gesture. "Olivia is Alex's best friend. She has every confidence in her. We love Annabelle, but I'd have to feel her future was in jeopardy to even suggest something like that. Olivia's doing everything possible—even going to baby classes. By herself, because Meg and Alex are both tied up tonight."

Brad tilted his chair back. *Baby class. Alone.* An opportunity for him to make her see it his way. In the kindest possible way, of course. Even if she didn't want him there.

"Are you sure there isn't more to this than your concern for Annabelle?"

He eyeballed Tom, the true do-gooder of the family. He'd been policing all their siblings' behavior since they were kids. Like when Brad and Kevin would be watching WWF wrestling and Tom would make them switch to PBS for Samantha. "What are you suggesting?"

"I don't know. Maybe you're a little harsh on Olivia because of your past."

Brad crossed his arms. "This has *nothing* to do with the past."

"She did leave you to go to New York for that scholarship. Maybe you've got a little pent-up resentment going on in there?" Tom tapped his head.

"I encouraged her to go." Because he was not going to be responsible for stopping her from achieving whatever she could. Even though he'd lost her in the process.

"You encouraged her but then you couldn't accept that she'd changed."

Brad scowled. "I was nineteen, Tom. I felt like my life was going nowhere. I felt trapped here. So I suppose you're right, I didn't handle that in the most mature way possible. But that's all water under the bridge. I'm just trying to do what's best for our brother's child."

"Maybe. But it sure sounds like you've got some unresolved feelings rolling around in that thick skull. And they're preventing you from focusing on what's important—Erika's fabulous tatas."

Brad laughed. "Nothing is going to stop me from doing that."

Tom pointed a finger. "You still have a thing for Olivia."

Brad snorted. "That was over a long time ago. It's just the construction stress."

"More like *Olivia* stress. You'd better be careful."

Brad shot him what he hoped was a *don't even go there* look. "Samantha's finally off at college. I'm thrilled to finally have my own place, and I'm loving every minute of it."

"Maybe. But Olivia's always been *The One Who Got Away* and now she's living next door. That's a fantasy most men just dream about."

"Trust me, I'm not lacking for women to dream about." Even though lately everyone in his dreams looked just like Olivia.

Something that would stop once he focused on the task at hand. In baby class, Olivia would be by herself, probably uncomfortable around all those expectant couples. Who wouldn't appreciate a partner, even if he was number one on her Do Not Invite list?

It wasn't too late for him to be the voice of reason. A little prodding on his part and he'd have Olivia realizing on her own what a ridiculously difficult job it was to raise a child, how her life wasn't set up to accommodate that. Then it would simply be a matter of time before she did the right thing for Annabelle.

Tom and Alex might give Olivia the benefit of the doubt and express their undying belief in her, but he was far more skeptical. He preferred not to leave things to fate.

"What time is it?" Brad rummaged under the papers until he found his phone. *Six fifteen.* He had just enough time to hightail it to the community center before class began. He'd still be back in plenty of time for his hot date at eight thirty. Standing up, he tucked his phone into his jeans pocket. "Gotta go."

"Whoa . . . what about laying the floor?"

"Rain check. I'm late for baby class."

He thought he heard Tom mumble something about it being plain crazy to be more excited about baby class than Erika's cleavage, but he didn't really care.

CHAPTER 7

"Go ahead and practice changing a diaper on your dolls," the smartly dressed woman at the front of the Community Center Health Education classroom instructed. From the doorway, Olivia glanced at the clock on the painted white brick wall. Class had begun ten minutes ago.

She'd been late dropping Annabelle off at Alex's because the baby had spit up all over her sweater. She'd changed, but just as she went to strap the baby in her car seat, Annabelle had done some business that needed changing ASAP.

Olivia released the door a little too early and it slammed shut behind her, causing twelve couples to look up from their seats at long rectangular tables. Every woman in the class was visibly pregnant.

What had she expected? This baby-care class was for soon-to-be parents, not a crash course for someone who had suddenly inherited a four-week-old. Olivia lifted her chin a little. What choice did she have? She needed help, and this was the place to get it. She took a deep breath and walked in.

"Welcome. I'm Dr. Bailey." The petite instructor, who had been talking to a couple in the first row, pointed to a vacant table in the center of the room. Much to Olivia's relief, Dr. Bailey wasn't pregnant too.

Olivia nodded and sought her seat, feeling chagrined that she'd already missed information she sorely needed. The last diaper she'd put on Annabelle had left a nasty red crease on her thigh. Not to mention the massive up-the-back accident that had made her late.

A life-sized doll lay in the middle of the table, along with a small stack of disposable diapers. Olivia sat, grabbed a diaper, and tucked it under her doll's bottom. After a little struggling, she taped one side but found it too loose. She pulled off the tape and readjusted, but it wouldn't hold anymore.

She was about to try again with a new diaper when she heard the click of the door. A tall, lean man entered in a T-shirt and jeans, a Yankees cap pulled down low on his forehead. A double take told her the worst.

Brad. The normal-guy clothing couldn't disguise his rock hard body, his confident saunter. A slow burn crept into her face. Their gazes clashed across the room, but she quickly busied herself with her task. What was he doing here, when she had specifically *un*invited him?

Suddenly Brad was next to her, scraping back an orange plastic chair and settling in like all he needed was a beer and a remote to feel more at home.

"Need any help?" His grin spread wider than a crooked car salesman's, immediately making her suspicious. Had he come to support her or show her up?

"Your head better?" he asked, casually sprawling his long legs under the table. He actually sounded concerned.

"Much, thanks."

"Well, you look a lot perkier."

She frowned. "Perkier? Cheerleaders are perky. *Breasts* are perky."

"Yes, they are." Brad's gaze dropped briefly to the V-neck of her gray sweater but she punched his arm hard enough to divert his gaze.

"Ow," he said in mock distress, rubbing his arm. "I just meant that you don't look like the blood-drained zombie you were before. Forgive my bad adjective."

He removed his cap, a big mistake. His dark hair hung in thick, precisely cut layers, still damp from a shower. When his extraordinary light green eyes sparkled, full of amiable good humor, an unwanted spark zinged straight to her groin. Why did he have to be the sexiest man she'd ever met?

The relationship book she was currently editing advised that no woman should ever date a "ten." "Tens" were full of themselves and had way more ego issues than your average nice-looking guy. Rather, the book advised, fall in love with an "eight" and give him a makeover.

She tried to tell herself that maybe Brad's nose was just a tad too big. Or his smile the tiniest bit crooked. But the truth was that every inch of his big, broad-shouldered, toned body tipped her personal hotness scale way past the "ten" side into the flushing, hot-flash, seeing-stars-and-fireworks-and-cartoon-explosions side. Her goose was so cooked . . .

Olivia bit down hard on her lip, hoping the pain would clear her senses. "Why are you here? I thought people in the restaurant business always worked evenings."

His smile floored her. Damn that dimple anyway. "Not tonight." His gaze drifted over her in a slow sweep. "Effie told me anyone without a significant other usually brings their mom. And I know you're the kind of person who would rather drown than ask for a lifeline."

"I'm perfectly capable . . ."

"It's not about capability, Sweetness." His mouth curved up in a lazy grin. "It's about not having to do something alone. I thought you might like some company, but I'll leave if you want me to."

"Oh." A parade of emotions skittered through her. Confusion. Wariness. Relief. Yes, it was a relief to have someone here with her amid all these happy pregnant couples. Even if he was the most irritating male in the world.

"So can I stay?" She hadn't known him as a young boy, but his innocent expression made her visualize a wide-eyed little tyke with freckles and a cowlick, exuding sincerity with a side of mischief from every pore. A pox on that hunky, handsome face that could still make her stomach turn cartwheels.

She nodded, but stopped short of thanking him. He stirred her, touched her, and she didn't trust that feeling at all. She pushed the doll toward Brad, happy to be rid of it. "Help yourself."

He put his hands up. "Hey, there, easy with our baby."

"It's not *real*." She rolled her eyes.

He pulled off the gnarled mess of twisted diaper and lifted it between them. "Besides, now that I'm here, I figured maybe you could use some guidance."

Give me a break. "I suppose you can do better." She passed him a fresh diaper.

He plucked it from her hand, but his fingers lingered over hers. "I do love me a challenge. Especially an easy one."

"You're awfully cocky," Olivia said. He was too close. His body heat radiated into her personal space and she smelled his cinnamon gum. But the assault to her senses was nothing compared to the way he looked at her—through her—clear past her neutral expression as if he saw every bit of the fear and self-doubt beneath. Instinctively, she pulled back.

"I'm skilled *and* cocky," Brad answered.

Olivia made a face. "What an ego. I don't remember it being so big."

"Honey, it's even bigger than it was before."

She felt herself blush again, but she was not going to let him get away with that. "But can it get the job done?"

His gaze raked her up and down, making her whole body feel like an August heat wave. She suddenly wished she could throw open the long row of pull-out windows for some cool evening air. In the seconds she was distracted by her hormonal flash, he had the diaper wrapped, taped, and tucked, neat as an Indian bunting.

"There you go." He shot her a wickedly pleased look.

"You cheated."

"Did not. How could I have cheated?"

"I don't know, but no one diapers anything that quickly."

"They do if they babysit my brother's kids all the time."

She poked him in the arm again, but his biceps were so taut her finger practically bounced. "Aha, so you *did* cheat."

"I've been trying to tell you, I have a lot more experience than I had in high school."

"Who doesn't?" she retorted.

"Ahem."

They both looked up to see Dr. Bailey standing in front of them. "We've moved on to the next topic," she whispered, not unkindly. "I'd suggest you two pay attention."

"Now you've gone and gotten us in trouble," Olivia said darkly.

"We're adults. We can't get in trouble for talking."

"Shhh. I have to listen."

"You always were teacher's pet."

She tossed him a glare to shut him up. The doctor showed Power-Point slides of bathing a baby.

"Why are you taking notes?" Brad whispered, his breath tickling her cheek. He grazed her shoulder with his warm, muscular one. Who could concentrate with those fresh soap and hot-blooded-man-body-spray smells assaulting her nostrils?

"Because I'm trying to learn something. Unlike *you*."

"Maybe I just know it all already."

"No crib bumpers," the doctor continued. "And always put the baby to sleep on her back because of SIDS risk."

Brad tipped backwards in his chair and raised his hand. "Doc, I imagine they get tired of being in the same position all the time."

"Well, it's up to you parents or caregivers to give babies time on their tummies when they're awake. If not, they can get plagiocephaly and have to wear a helmet."

"Plag—e—o—what?" a father-to-be asked from the front row.

Brad interjected. "It's when they develop flat spots on their heads."

"Who's teacher's pet now?" Olivia grumbled. "Or are you just trying to get in her pants?"

Brad displayed an expression of mock shock. "How could you even think that of me? I'm offended."

"Why do you live to irritate me?"

His green eyes twinkled. "Because it's fun."

"Take a look at the samples of formula in front of you," Dr. Bailey continued. "One is a liquid concentrate, one is ready to use, and one is a powder."

Olivia looked at the various-sized containers. She'd had no idea there were so many choices.

"Here in Mirror Lake, we have to be sure to use low-fluoride water. Can anyone tell us why?"

Olivia's stomach turned a tumble. She'd been using water straight from the tap. Her hand began to shake as she took notes.

The doctor's words ran together. Olivia'd totally missed that part about the fluoride, still in a panic about using tap water. Had she done something bad to Annabelle in some way she wasn't even aware of? She didn't even know the basics about caring for a child.

A slide flashed by about cutting fingernails. How on earth would she ever manage to hold Annabelle's tiny fingers still? She shuddered again when she thought of the cute bumpers around Annabelle's mattress. Those would have to go, too. What else didn't she know?

A big hand covered her own. "You all right?" Brad asked. His eyes were warm with concern. Or fake concern, she couldn't tell.

Olivia swallowed past the baseball clogging her throat. "I-I didn't know to use special water. Or boil new bottles. We didn't do that in the grocery store, we just ripped open the package and—"

Brad squeezed her hand. His touch was firm and gentle all at once. "She'll be fine, Olivia. It's just a precaution. And that was an emergency."

It was all so complicated. Dangers lurked everywhere. She didn't need an evening class, she needed a graduate seminar. Tears pricked at the backs of her eyes.

"Raising a child is a scary business," Brad said. "Even for two parents who have a support system of family nearby," Brad said. His voice was gentle but his message rankled.

I'm not good enough. I never will be. The grim reality seeped into her bones like a damp chill. Maternal instincts apparently hadn't made it into her genetic code.

Once she went back to New York, she was on her own, responsible for an infant she hadn't read the instruction manual on. And the warranty would be expired. There was no going back.

"It doesn't have to be like this," Brad continued. "Maybe you need to think about what's best for Annabelle."

That startled her. When had she not thought of Annabelle? "Wh-what do you mean?"

"What I mean is you're always so independent, so take-charge. Maybe in this instance that's not the best thing."

She frowned. Her stomach gave a nauseating churn. He was calling into question her ability to mother Annabelle. That wasn't new. But what if he was right?

"I'm saying give it a try, see what happens, but you've got a safety net if it doesn't work out."

"I'm not getting what you're saying." Was he being his usual annoying self, or was he seeing some cold, hard truth she could not even admit to herself?

"Tom and Alex would never interfere with what you want. But they'd be there if you felt it wasn't going to work out."

"Have they . . . said something to you?"

"Of course not. But they love Annabelle, too, and I have a feeling they wouldn't hesitate to take her if you felt you couldn't."

She wished she could say that her caring for Annabelle was what her sister intended, but in her heart, she didn't believe that. Somehow, her name had gotten written in on the wills. As a whim, perhaps. In the space that said "next of kin," her sister probably scratched it in and got Kevin to do the same, never imagining this nightmare would come to fruition.

He squeezed her hand again. "You'll make the right decision. And as for the bottles, Annabelle will be fine. No reason to panic."

Olivia drew in a deep breath. She had to get a grip. He was right. The baby was fine, no harm was done. "I'm sorry. I'm just a little . . . overwhelmed."

"You'll work it out."

His sure and confident tone didn't comfort her frayed nerves. As class ended, she packed up the diaper bag with the Mirror Lake Community Hospital logo on it that everyone received for free. Brad handed her the diapers and the formula.

"You know, it's a little odd, having the tables turned like this," he said.

"What do you mean?"

"Well, you were always the perfect one. Straight As, full scholarship to NYU. I was lucky to graduate."

She stopped packing the bag. "You worked three jobs to support your family. And used to drink four cups of coffee every morning just to stay awake in class."

He rubbed the back of his neck, as uncomfortable with praise as he'd been years ago. "There wasn't much time back then for books—or leisure. But I'm making up for it now."

Women were surely lined up clear to Hartford to date him. Olivia remembered a recent style magazine article featuring up-and-coming entrepreneurs. It had chronicled Brad's lifestyle, the fact that he supported his hometown—and his state—but also traveled internationally to explore new menu ideas. There was a photo spread of him in Greece, his arm wrapped around a stunning woman who was probably a model. Yes, he took his leisure, all right.

The table was clear. Brad replaced his cap on his head. "Well, I've got to be going."

Panic welled up fresh inside her. Not that Brad was especially comforting but the thought of being left alone with Annabelle suddenly terrified the living daylights out of her. "Wait," she called after him. "How did you know so much about everything? It must've involved more than babysitting."

"Tom and Alex read every baby book known to man before they had their first kid. When I babysat, I guess I got bored and read a couple of them."

"Oh." The hottest bachelor in Mirror Lake babysat and read parenting how-to books. Who'd have figured?

Awkward silence descended. For once Olivia couldn't think of a barb to jab him with, or a quip to get his goat.

"See you around," Brad said cordially—too nicely. She wished they were joking lightly like before. She would rile him up enough, and he would zing her back with some smartass remark. But the mood had shifted. Without another word, he turned and walked his fine backside up the aisle and out the rec center door.

As Olivia slung the bag over her shoulder and made her own way out, she realized coming to baby class hadn't helped at all. It only underscored how much she still had to learn.

CHAPTER 8

Erika Peters lightly scraped a path down Brad's arm with her long purple-painted nails. "I've really been looking forward to our date." Her exotic scent wafted across the lakeside table at his restaurant, mixing with the spectacular entrees in front of them in a slightly unpleasant way that made Brad's normally stone-cast stomach lurch a little.

Perfume mixed with seared sea scallops was just off.

Olivia always smelled simpler. Like baby lotion and lemons. Tonight she'd worn a plain gray sweater and her hair had been done up in a messy bun, but she somehow managed to look sexy as hell. Erika, on the other hand, was Cosmo caliber in every way: shiny black hair in a smooth twist, smoky eyes, glossy lips. And the deep plunge of her clingy gown indicated the light was green for a night of hot sex. *Lots* of it.

The new expansion to the restaurant looked spectacular, even though it was still roped off. The deck was lit by twinkly white lights strung in bushes and potted plants and crisscrossed between wooden posts. Outdoor heaters chased away the slight chill and a fire burned in the new outdoor fireplace. Couples gathered round, watching a big crimson sun set quietly over the water. In the distance, jumping fish gave an occasional splash, and the scent of lilacs from the town square wafted in on a light breeze.

Just a few days ago, Brad would have considered himself damn lucky to sit across the table from such a gorgeous woman on a perfect evening like this. They'd been flirting for weeks, and tonight was the night to make things happen.

But things weren't perfect. All he could think of was that damn baby class. Olivia had listened so carefully, even took notes. She'd been visibly upset and a bit overwhelmed.

Every instinct had compelled him to pull her into his arms and comfort her. But instead he'd fed her some malarkey about not being so independent, asking for help, doing what was best for Annabelle.

That was his intention, right? To dissuade her. Get her to think of alternatives. Capitalize on her vulnerabilities. He certainly hadn't gone to class for her. Had he?

No. Of course he hadn't.

Yet the thought of her going through everything alone, after all that had happened, made his stomach lurch. Every parent had a learning curve. Hers was just steep and fast and frightening, like the giant slide at the water park.

And he'd given her a shove down when she was already anxious.

He hadn't even had to be mean. He could have pointed out that she'd had a poor role model as a mother. Or that Trish and Kevin hadn't really thought this whole cockamamie plan out. But she'd done the self-flagellating all by herself.

And he'd stood by and watched it happen. Like the total donkey's behind that he was.

He could see how hard she was trying, with no one nearby to encourage her. She was truly on her own. He could have rectified that, but he'd chosen to stay silent.

For the first time, Brad acknowledged with a sickening sense of fear that getting close to Olivia would only ignite those unstable feelings that bubbled below the surface in every conversation, every argument, waiting for some small catalyst to combust into an unstoppable, volatile explosion.

"I know how busy you've been with renovations, but I'm so glad we took time to meet tonight," Erika said. "And I've got great news. Marc Daniels is coming to judge Bachelors Who Cook, and he wants to film an episode of his cooking show right here in Mirror Lake. At your restaurant. Isn't that exciting?"

Brad jerked his head up. "Marc Daniels, the celebrity chef?" Who hosted a cooking show on Food Network, and owned several five-star restaurants in New York City. He would be a huge boon for their event, which in turn would be great for the hospital and great for his restaurant. The B and Bs, the lakefront, and the downtown would be packed.

Erika pressed her white teeth into her lower lip and smiled. "Yep. Mirror Lake is going to be on national television, and the crowds he attracts will be huge."

She reached across the table and grasped Brad's hands. As she leaned over, he caught an excellent view of her ample cleavage. The tiny candle in the center of the table flickered off her high-cheekboned face, drawing attention to a provocative little mole at the side of her mouth.

Traditionally, this was the time he'd go in for the kill. Stroke her lovely fingers, use a playful tug to pull her in closer, then whisper something sexy in her ear. But he wasn't feeling it.

Thrown off his game, Brad glanced away. A moving figure at the edge of his vision caught his eye—his sister-in-law Alex, sitting down at a table about twenty feet away, near the edge of the water. With Olivia.

Olivia?

She pulled out a chair. An uncomfortable feeling settled in Brad's stomach, and he fought a sudden urge to run over to their table and welcome them. It shocked him to realize he wanted Olivia's first time at his restaurant to be with him, not Alex. He wanted to show her everything he'd done to it since it was little more than a greasy-spoon fried seafood chain.

"Brad? Are you all right?" Erika swept a lock of long dark hair behind her ear. She licked her bold red lips. "You seem . . . distracted."

Brad tore his gaze off Olivia and forced himself into small talk with Erika, who smiled her megawatt smile that thrilled thousands of viewers nightly on Channel Five, but nothing happened—no tingling, no fireworks. He must be more tired than he thought.

Out of the corner of his eye, he watched Olivia order off the menu. One of the newest waiters took her order. Would he know to tell her a fresh shipment of crawfish had just arrived from the Gulf today and his chef's gumbo was to die for?

He had to stop this. There was nothing he could offer her beyond some really hot sex. Their attraction would go nowhere. She was headed back to New York soon and there was no way he was going to allow her to take his heart with her—again.

But dammit, he wanted her. This was all due to the lack of sex. And his best opportunity to get some was sitting inches away.

He turned back to Erika. She waited in a posture of anticipation, eager for him to say the word. *One tiny word* was all it would take to trade in his frustrations for a night of pure, raw pleasure.

He stared at her beautiful face. Opened his mouth.

"I'll be right back." The wrong words tumbled out, but for him they were exactly right. Brad scraped back his chair and walked over to Olivia's table, patted the waiter on his back and stepped up in his place. He had a million things to tell her, but all that came out was, "Try the gumbo. It's Phillipe's new recipe and it will knock your socks off. The angel hair shrimp is also fabulous if you like pasta."

Olivia greeted him politely but her eyes told him she was wary. Upset.

"We just came for a quick bite," Alex explained. "Annabelle fell asleep and Tom offered to watch her for an hour."

Brad nodded but couldn't capture Olivia's gaze. "I'm glad you ladies came. Enjoy your dinner."

He ran back to his own table. "Ready for dessert?" he asked.

Erika tossed him a scorching glance. "I thought we could have dessert at my place, if you know what I mean."

Brad managed a half smile. The woman was offering herself up on a platter.

Erika smiled sympathetically. Her shiny purple nails tapped the glass of the table. "I can tell you have a lot on your mind, but I want you to know I'm here to help. There's been a vibe between us for weeks now. I'm not shy about admitting it." She reached over and covered his hand with hers.

Dammit. It was now or never. Brad looked over Erika's shoulder. Olivia was chatting away with Alex, too far away to hear anything. Why did it matter if she did?

He was so hosed. He didn't know why, but it *did* matter. *She* mattered.

For Annabelle's sake. For her future. *That was all.*

Brad gathered up Erika's pretty hands. "You're right. About my being distracted. A lot has happened these few weeks and I . . . I need some time. That's not to say you aren't an amazing, incredible woman."

Erika pulled away. Her laugh was soft and sultry like the rest of her. "When men start using words like *amazing* and *incredible*, you know there's trouble. I know you've been through a lot. I just wanted to . . . offer you comfort."

"I appreciate it. But I've got to say no."

He finally managed a glance at Olivia's table.

Empty.

But they hadn't gotten past salad. Had something happened, maybe to Annabelle?

He excused himself from his ruined date and punched a number into his cell. "What happened?" he asked Alex.

"A better question is, what the hell happened in baby class?"

"Nothing." Brad paused. "Okay, maybe something did. But I'm going to fix it. I've got to go."

Relieved that Annabelle was okay, Brad stopped briefly in the kitchen to tell his staff he'd be back at 8:00 a. m.

In his car, Brad slammed his hands on the steering wheel and cursed. No matter what he told himself, Olivia wasn't a fleeting, temporary memory from an innocent time long past. She was as deeply entrenched in him as the massive roots of the centuries-old beech trees in the town square. It appeared he was as incapable of undermining her as he was of forgetting her.

He couldn't stand her feeling badly because of him. He wanted to apologize. Be her advocate instead of her enemy. He couldn't give her anything else, but he could at least give her that.

As he headed out of the lot, he couldn't believe he'd just chosen complicated, full-of-trouble, give-him-grief Olivia over all-I-want-is-sex Erika.

CHAPTER 9

The incessant knocking forced Olivia to come to the door even though she wanted company about as much as she wanted her wisdom teeth pulled. Brad stood propped on the other side, his thick crop of hair and the tip of his nose pressed against the screen, making for a scary sight. She smoothed down her old gray T-shirt, covered with water blotches from Annabelle's bath. "It's been a long day. I'm really not up for company."

"I come bearing food." He dangled a cardboard take-out box in front of her. "And something to wash it down with." He produced two icy cold bottles of beer from behind his back. He looked at her with a hopeful expression. "Now will you let me in?"

"Brad, I'm really tired. I'm afraid I'm going to have to take a rain check." Something smelled really amazing in those cartons but no way was she going to show any further weakness in front of him today, even for something as elemental as hunger. Her stomach betrayed her by growling loudly in protest.

"Actually, the food is just a peace offering. I came over to talk with you." He paused. "Please." His eyes held a soft, penitent look that mushed up her insides a little and almost got to her.

Olivia cast him a wary glance. "I don't want any more advice about what I should do for Annabelle." Her gut was still all twisted up about that. She hadn't even been able to eat dinner with Alex.

He grinned widely. "No more advice. I promise." He pushed open the screen and strode through the doorway, handing her the beers and setting the take-out containers on the small kitchen table, which stood between the kitchen and family room.

He wore a T-shirt and athletic shorts, and his feet were bare. As he made himself at home, finding plates and silverware, Olivia did not want to notice the broad chest that tapered down to a lean waist or his tanned legs full of rock-hard muscle, covered with the same light coat of bronze hair she'd seen on his arms. He looked as delicious as the food smelled.

But looks were deceiving. He had his own agenda to push and it was the opposite of hers. She was exhausted and upset and fed up and she would not allow sex hormones to rule her body.

He turned from the table, his gaze raking her with a slow sweep. He lifted one well-defined brow. "Wow, what happened to you? Water fight?"

Olivia looked down at her shirt. A water stain revealed the outline of her bra and *oh, God*, was that a nipple perking up? She quickly peeled the shirt away from her skin. "I'm sure you'd like to show me how fast you can bathe a baby without spilling a drop of water but I'm tired."

Brad's Adam's apple rolled in his neck. He stared at her breast. Maybe she wasn't the only one whose hormones were firing out of line.

Olivia crossed her hands over her chest.

"I'm not here to criticize you, Olivia." Brad cleared his throat, took a glance around at the kitchen. A hot mess abounded—baby bottles, a heap of towels and baby clothes, a pile of mail her boss had forwarded from work. Once she'd edited a book called *A Hundred Ways to Keep Clutter at Bay*. Too bad she hadn't had any time to put even one into effect.

Brad leveled his gaze directly at her. "You left before dinner."

What a bad idea that had been, to follow Alex's lead to go to Brad's restaurant. But it had seemed safe, as he'd said he wasn't going to be there. How was she supposed to know he was taking Ms. Hottie Reporter to his restaurant on a date? She must be someone special if he'd brought her to the place that was so obviously his pride and joy. Worse, how was Olivia supposed to explain why she'd left? She'd already used up the headache excuse for today.

Olivia's mouth ran, working overtime to fill up the uncomfortable space between them. "Rosie lost her doll again, so Alex left before it turned into a crisis." She flicked her wrist nonchalantly. "You know how it is, kids and all." Over her dead body would she admit stress as an excuse for leaving. "Your restaurant is really beautiful, though."

Brad took a step closer. His rich cologne tickled her nostrils. And something more, a scent that was exclusively *him* that was familiar and strangely comforting. "I'm sorry you didn't get to stay longer for the whole experience."

"Yeah, well, maybe next time." He was still staring. "Look, you've made your point already. You didn't need to come over here to reinforce it, to bribe me with food and pretend to be nice." She could not risk falling for him again. Or allow him to comfort her when he clearly had a bigger agenda. So she backed up too fast, her heel smacking into the base of a kitchen cabinet. Maybe the impact jarred something loose inside her brain, because suddenly she had to tell it like it was.

Rubbing her injured foot, she continued, "Let's face it. I'm a single woman with a demanding job who inherited an infant I haven't got a clue about taking care of, and I think it was probably an accident that my name got put on the will."

Olivia inhaled deeply in an attempt at control. She should've stopped right then, but the more she tried to hold back, the more her anger flared. "I'll tell you one thing, Brad Rushford, you big hulking know-it-all"—she stabbed him in the chest with her index finger—"one thing growing up without a mother taught me. That was to be independent and to know my own mind, because I knew no one was going to defend me or pick me up when I fell or kiss my booboos. I had to rely on myself.

"So regardless of how much you fight me, you can't take away one simple fact. I love this baby. From the moment Alex put her in my arms and I saw her tiny helpless face, I knew I would do whatever it takes to give her a great life. A fantastic life. And I don't know if my sister truly had the faith in me to do this, but I loved her with all my heart and I swear to God I will love and cherish her baby forever. So you can stop judging me and leave me be."

Olivia clamped her hand over her eyes because tears were streaming down her face like rivulets of rain down a windshield. A great sob shook her. She moved to back away from him, to flee the kitchen, but Brad grasped her by the arms and dragged her solidly against his big broad chest. Initially she fought him, but he was built of solid rock and she wasn't going anywhere. One hand stroked her head as if she were a child while the other made tiny circles on her back. "Shhh," he said. "It's all right. I miss them, too."

Against her will, she gave in, because sharing the burden of her grief was the greatest comfort she'd experienced since her sister died. She wanted to stay like that forever, drawing solace and strength from his big body. But she didn't trust him. Not at all. So she made herself push away. "Let go of me. You've been trying to undermine me since I came."

He loosened his hold but didn't let go. "You're right. And I'm sorry."

She stilled. The fight drained out of her like a fizzling balloon. Did she hear him correctly? "Why are you suddenly changing your tune?"

"I thought I knew what was best for Annabelle. I was wrong."

"And now you suddenly believe that I'm the right person to mother that baby?"

He traced a tear with his finger, cupped her face in his big strong hands. His eyes filled with raw tenderness and, God help her, she felt the truth of that look through to her bones. "You've always been so hard on yourself," he said. "Most people have nine months to get used to the idea of having a baby and you've had two days. Give yourself a break."

A huge avalanche of relief broke over her and dammit, she cried even more.

No one moved. For a suspended second, the clock drew out one slow tick at a time. Brad's cool green eyes filled up with heat, his gaze drilling down on her as if she were dinner.

She could not look away. But she had to, before they crossed over into a moment that would stretch from awkward to just plain weird. "We should probably eat before it gets cold."

Brad shook his head.

"You're not hungry?" she asked, her heart stumbling.

He smiled, slow and wide and predatory. A glint gleamed in his eyes. "Oh, I'm hungry, all right."

She gasped. Her skin flooded with heat. Instinct caused her to try and flee but it was impossible to move.

"Eat later," he said, cupping her neck with his hand and pulling her close as he covered her lips with his.

He devoured her with wet, deep kisses, tangling their tongues as he plunged deep. An uncontrollable moan that sounded nothing at all like her voice left her lips as she met him stroke for stroke. He took hold of her face, angling it for ultimate possession. Their bodies locked into place, flush against each other, all her soft curves against his hard, unrelenting ones. He felt so damn good and tasted so delicious, her knees buckled. In one fell swoop, Brad nudged her a few steps backwards until they both toppled onto the family room couch.

He smoothed a rough hand down her cheeks, gently pushing the unruly curls away. His face was inches away, and she got lost in those amazing green eyes that contained a softness akin to the way he looked at Annabelle. And yet different, mixed with a raw, primitive wanting that turned her blood to liquid heat. "I want you," he said roughly.

She reached up her hands to encircle his wrists and met his eyes, which were dangerous and dark with need. His pulse throbbed hard and fast beneath her fingertips, and it thrilled her to know how intensely she affected him. Rendered speechless, her breath coming in choppy gasps, all she could do was nod helplessly.

Leaving no room for hesitation, he took her mouth again, teasing his tongue in and out, tasting her, pausing only long enough to whisk off his shirt and help her with hers. His erection strained against her, demanding and large. She clawed at the flexing muscles of his back, trying to pull him down to feel the delicious pressure of his body over hers.

Her worry and confusion fled like fireflies into the warm evening, the void replaced by a flood of desire. She wanted him. God, she wanted him, ten thousand times more than ever before.

Olivia traced the waistband of his shorts, roved over the taut muscle of his lean hips, tugged on the button of his shorts until it popped open, and threaded her fingers under his briefs. His hands skimmed her waist, her back, even as his mouth continued its path down her trembling flesh. His lips were everywhere, searing a trail of heat along her stomach, her hip, her navel.

He was the same, yet totally different, this man she'd known intimately from so long ago. Loaded with confidence and the secret knowledge of exactly what she wanted, he was all raw sexual energy, animal heat, and total skyrocketing hotness.

A voice penetrated the screen door and their sexual haze. "Oh my God, what is going on in there? Brad, is that you?"

Olivia's hands froze. Brad tore his lips from hers and turned to the door, using his body like a shield. "Alex? What are you doing here?" he growled.

His twisting movement caused Olivia to tumble to the floor. She dashed a shirt over her head. Alex walked in, the screen door smacking its frame like a scold. She glared at Brad. "I thought Olivia was being attacked."

Yeah, right. Olivia knew exactly what she thought, and exactly why she'd barged in. To stop her from making a huge mistake.

Between her bedraggled hair and the oversized tee—dammit, she'd grabbed Brad's by mistake—she knew exactly what she must look like. Like they'd been having sex all night. The shock and horror she felt was mirrored in Alex's face.

Alex descended on Brad like a mother hen. "Tom told me it sounded as if you were thinking of teaching Olivia a lesson at baby class. And I ran into Jeanine Peterson in Gertie's. She said you were the only guy in the class who knew what *plagiocephaly* was. Is that true?" She poked a finger in his chest. "And now you're taking advantage of my best friend when she's at her most vulnerable."

"Alex, please. You're overreacting," Olivia said.

Alex stood unrelenting, hands on hips. "Ask him, Olivia. Just ask him."

"He came to baby class to help out. So I would have a partner." Olivia met his gaze but his eyes immediately dropped. "Didn't you?"

Brad exhaled sharply and ran a hand through his hair. His hesitation spoke louder than words.

Olivia narrowed her eyes. "You purposely came to make me feel insecure, more than I already am?"

"Let me explain," Brad said.

"We're waiting," Alex said, tapping her toe like an impatient schoolmarm.

His gaze, usually so direct, shifted downward like a guilty schoolboy's. "I admit I wanted to get you to see my side. But I meant everything I just said, Olivia. I understand you feel upset and confused and—"

Upset? Confused? It sounded so demeaning. "So you'd capitalize on my confusion even further to *get me into bed*?"

"No! That was just hormones."

"Just *hormones*?" She picked up the nearest object—her flip-flop—and tossed it at his head. It hit him in the ear. "Get out."

"Alex is rabble-rousing." Brad shot Alex a deadly glare. "I can explain."

Olivia shook her head. "Alex is *protecting* me. Please leave."

And for the final cherry on top of the whole ugly scene, the baby let out a very unhappy wail.

⊷──◦──⊶

"Are you all right?" Alex asked sometime later. She handed Olivia a cup of chamomile tea, Trish's favorite, and sat down next to Olivia on the couch.

"Considering I almost had sex with my ex, and he's a sleazeball, yes and no."

"Oh, honey." She sat down beside her. "Maybe I shouldn't have come. I tried your cell, but you weren't answering."

"Trust me, I'm glad you came. I almost made the mistake of a lifetime." Visions filled her head of a toddler-sized Annabelle opening a Christmas present from Uncle Brad and Aunt Kardashian while she looked on, gritting her teeth and praying for the holiday to be over. "Thank God you came."

Olivia sipped the tea, took cleansing breaths. *It was okay. It wasn't too late.* "He was so nice. He brought dinner, we chatted like old times . . ."

"It's Brad turning on his charm."

God, she'd been so stupid. She was almost thirty years old, yet she acted like a naïve teenager again, trusting him when she never, ever should have. "I never thought he'd stoop to that level."

"Brad is a good man, Olivia. But this is going too far. Look, I do not expect you to come to the picnic tomorrow."

The picnic. All the Rushfords would be there. When she told Alex she'd made a date to have dinner with her dad, she'd invited him, too.

"No." She was not about to drop her tail between her legs and skip. "I want to see everyone and I want to bring Annabelle."

She'd show him she was competent to mother this baby, and she'd make him regret the day he ever tried to mess with her.

CHAPTER 10

"You broke the code of the Brotherhood," Brad said as he sat on the picnic table, drinking a beer and watching Tom rotate chicken breasts on his new outdoor grill. He scanned the yard, with its big old trees dotting a green slope of grass that led down to the lake. His family was gathered on the big deck, enjoying cold drinks and talking. The midday sun was hot and sweet, perfect for the first Rushford picnic of the season.

But Olivia wasn't there. She'd ignored his calls. She probably wouldn't even show today.

Guilt pummeled him. He'd been an idiot to try to make her feel bad.

"Sometimes you've got to choose between brotherhood and marriage-hood." Tom said as he stopped poking at the chicken and closed the grill lid.

"Sex was involved, wasn't it?" Brad asked.

"Something like that." Tom's smile—and the candy pink hearts on his black apron—dulled the intimidation factor of his large frame.

"All I said was you were a little too eager to get to baby class. She figured out the rest."

Alex stepped down from the sliding patio door and crossed the deck. Even on her day off she looked classy in red walking shorts and a navy polo. She tossed both of them a glare. "Here's the chicken. And so help me Brad, I don't want any trouble with Olivia today."

Tom took the chicken from his wife and tapped her playfully on the derriere.

She swatted his hand away in mock annoyance. "Mind your manners—your grandma's watching." She honed in on Brad. "The whole family's here, including Olivia's dad. So best behavior, is that clear?"

Great. Frank Marks would find a way to stick more burrs in his side, for sure. But he'd handle it. Brad saluted. "Aye, Captain."

Alex put her hands on her hips. "If only you used that smarty-pants business brain of yours, you'd realize that helping Olivia would be a whole lot better than antagonizing her."

"I'm not as much of an asshole as you think." He actually didn't care so much what Alex thought of him—but he did want to make things right with Olivia. That's why he'd gone over there last night, before things got out of control. One look at her liquid chocolate eyes and her tight little ass and every caveman instinct he possessed came hurtling out, all reason tossed out the window. He should never have let that happen.

And it wouldn't happen again. She was leaving soon and it would be foolish to start something. He would keep his distance, be cordial, and somehow live through this next week and a half without touching her again.

The sound of laughter made Brad turn his head. In the wide expanse of yard, someone had dragged out two beanbag-toss boards. His youngest brother Benjamin stooped over one of them, deep in discussion with a woman—no doubt his date. Usually Ben brought a different girlfriend to every picnic all summer long.

This one was a looker, too. Dark hair bound up in a thick ponytail. White shorts that showed off pretty, fit legs, and a bright pink top. They were gesturing animatedly to the game boards and laughing. The woman playfully pushed Ben and he pretended to topple over. As she bent to pick up a beanbag, Brad did a double take.

Olivia? No way. But where was Annabelle? He craned his neck around to the deck behind him. Effie sat in an Adirondack chair, cooing to the baby.

Brad's body tensed and grew rigid. His beer almost spilled. Ben had been no more than a skinny little punk when Olivia had left, but now he was a newly graduated doctor, not to mention a young single guy on the prowl.

He'd damn well better not be prowling after her.

"Okay, okay," Ben said. "I'll give you the point."

"You will not," Olivia countered. "I'll *take* it because I earned it."

"Your bag's halfway off the board."

"It's halfway *on* the board. Rules say that's one point." They stood toe-to-toe, but the top of Olivia's head only came up to Ben's chest. "Listen, Squirt, rules are rules. On the board is on the board."

Ben laughed. He'd grown a beard, making him look more mature than twenty-seven. "How can you call me Squirt when I'm six four now?"

Six four and a lady killer. The best looking of all the brothers. Before he could think, Brad jumped off the table and stalked across the yard.

Olivia put her hands on her hips in mock irritation. She looked pretty, and for the first time since she'd returned to town, she reminded Brad of the fresh-faced teenager she'd been, full of smiles and a lightheartedness that had clearly gone missing.

"Benjamin," she said in a teasing tone, "I remember you when you were an annoying fifteen-year-old with a bad case of acne and a crush on Amanda Bynes. You used to watch *What I Like About You* in secret in the basement."

"Yeah, well, you haven't got anything on me. I can tell a good story or two about you and my brother sneaking around—"

Brad cleared his throat. "I know how to figure out whose point it is."

Surprise lit up Olivia's face, replaced quickly by irritation.

He talked fast before she could tell him to get the hell out of Dodge. "Rules say if you can lift the board without the bag falling off, it counts as a point." He walked over to the board and pulled it straight up. The bag stayed on the edge. "Olivia's point," he pronounced.

Olivia walked by him and whispered something as she bent down to pick up the bag. It sounded like "ass kiss."

He grinned, probably from the sheer fact that she was *talking* to him. "I mean," he said in a low voice, "that would be a big sacrifice, but if that's what it takes so you're not angry with me, so be it."

She didn't smile. "Try an apology."

Ben was clueless as to anything out of the ordinary going on. "I demand a rematch."

"I'm in on this round," Brad said quickly.

Ben cupped his hands over his mouth and called out. "Alex, get your hiney over here. One short round so I can get my honor back."

Alex called from the deck, "I'm glad you all are playing but somebody's got to get this picnic together."

"I'll come help you." Olivia moved to leave.

"Stay." Ben held her back and yelled up to Alex, "One short round, then we'll all help get the food out. Come on down here."

Brad tugged at Olivia's free arm. "We'll go on this side. Girls against boys." She tensed under his touch. "Okay?"

"Whatever," she said, pulling her arm back.

Alex joined them, and she and Ben took turns tossing.

"Ben certainly grew up," Olivia remarked.

"Nah. He's the same pain in the ass as always," Brad said.

"Has he got a girlfriend?"

"Why? You interested?" He knew that sounded snarky, but he couldn't help it.

Olivia laughed. What was so funny about that?

"I just wondered why he and Meg never got together. She's had a huge crush on him since forever."

Brad picked up the bags. "Meg's far too good for that rangy mutt."

Why was he so relieved she wasn't interested in his baby brother? "You go first."

Their fingers accidentally touched as she grabbed the bag. A sizzling snap of a pulse jolted up his arm. He wished they were alone. He'd drag her down into the sweet, dandelion-speckled lawn in the perfect sunshine of this day and make both of them forget all about loss and babies without parents and difficult decisions. Those few moments with her last night were brief, but enough to let him know how good it would be between them. Amazing. Just like it had been before.

What was she doing to him? A few minutes in her presence and his resolve shattered as easily as a thin coating of ice.

Olivia's throw went wide. Someone let the dog out of the house, a big yellow lab mix that immediately bolted over to the bag and snatched it up in his mouth.

Olivia ran to the dog but he dodged her, staying just out of reach and chewing happily on the bag. Soon it would be ripped to shreds.

"Rex! Drop that bag right now. Pronto," Alex commanded her dog-child.

The dog shook his head as if to say "no way," sinking his teeth further into the bag, and ran off toward the woods.

"Smart dog." Olivia giggled.

Brad ran over to the grill and lifted a piece of cooked chicken from a platter. "Come here, Rex. Come here, boy."

Brad dangled the meat as he cajoled the dog. Rex swiftly dropped the mangled bag, trotted over and scarfed up the chicken. Brad swooped up the bag. "Well, I guess beanbag

toss is over for the day."

"Maybe permanently from the looks of it," Olivia said. "Sorry about the bag."

"We win." Ben grinned and gave her ponytail a yank. An innocent gesture, but it made Brad fist his hand in a simmering fury.

Hands. Off. She's. Mine.

Brad tried to walk with Olivia back up to the house but she was already walking with Ben, laughing and teasing like before.

"It didn't take them long to reconnect. Just like old times," Alex said.

Brad scowled. "Except my brother is a man now."

Alex raised an elegant brow. "Does that disturb you?"

Before Brad could answer, a little girl with pigtails ran across the yard to Alex. She tapped on her mother's leg impatiently. "Mommy, I want to see my new cousin. Hi, Uncy Brad."

Brad bent down and scooped the little girl up in his arms. "Hey there, Rosie. I'm a little hungry. Can I have a snack?"

A cascade of giggles erupted from the child. "What kinda snack do you want?"

"Little girl snack!" Brad pretended to gnaw on her arm as she shrieked with laughter. Then he flipped her over and set her down on the ground.

"Uncy Brad, lift me up," the four-year-old demanded, her arms hiked up. "I wanna go see Annybelle."

Brad complied, and walked over to where Tom stood flipping burgers and talking with Olivia.

". . . missed my curfew. Brad was on a date with you. I still remember him stalking up to my old jalopy with a flashlight and pulling me out of there by the neck. Scared the crap out of me. Not to mention my date."

"And you never took anybody parking at the airport again after that," Brad said.

Tom pointed the barbecue tongs at his brother and laughed. "Not after curfew, I didn't."

Annabelle was dressed in a little flowered one-piece thing. She even wore a hat on her head and little matching socks, although one was kicked halfway off. Brad had to admit, things looked under control. Even Olivia looked better. Still a little tired, but she had a trace of a tan now, and she wore a pair of pink and green dangly earrings that sparkled in the sun. Frivolous. Fun. A whole different side of her.

Olivia pushed Annabelle's hat back so Rosie could see better. The little girl gently touched the baby's arm and cast an admiring look.

"I wuv the baby, Auntie Liv. I wish you didn't have to go back to New York."

Olivia paused, clearly taken aback. "New York's not so far, Rosie. You'll see your cousin lots, don't worry."

Brad's heart twisted. Would Annabelle get the chance to cavort around and play on the swing set with her cousins, join in the whiffle ball and dodgeball and water balloon tournaments? Or would she become a city girl, more accustomed to Central Park romps and dutiful, but uncomfortable, visits out to the country once or twice a year?

He set Rosie down to run off and find her little brothers.

"Speaking of Rushford siblings," Olivia said, "I don't see Samantha anywhere."

"She's in Boston working on a research project for the summer. She studies psychology." Brad couldn't keep the pride from his voice. At last, his sister appeared to be on the right track, being mentored by a renowned professor who was supervising her project. And she'd finally gotten those foolish ideas about art school out of her head.

Brad squatted next to Olivia's lawn chair. Absently, he pushed Annabelle's sock more securely onto her foot. "I need to talk to you about a few things. I—"

"Hey, Olivia, heard you had a meltdown in the grocery store the other day," Benjamin teased.

Hands down, Brad would say he possessed the most irritating family in the world. "That was the baby, not Olivia, you dumbass."

"Chill, bro, she knows I'm just teasing."

Olivia kissed Annabelle's forehead. Annabelle regarded her seriously with round saucer eyes. "We're doing better now."

"Can I talk to you?" Brad asked.

"Sure, sweetheart, any time," Ben answered in a mocking voice only a sibling could master so well.

"Benjamin, get the hell out of here."

The murderous look Brad impaled him with must have gotten the message across, because Ben threw up his hands and backed away. "I'm going, I'm going."

"Would you two mind bringing out the side dishes?" Alex said, carrying a platter of meat. "They're all on the kitchen table."

"Sure, of course." Olivia rose without waiting for him and walked across the deck to the house, handing Annabelle off to Effie again. Brad couldn't help but notice her shapely behind filling out those white shorts. He let his gaze slide down her long, smooth legs. He bet they'd feel as silky as they looked. Each of her flip-flops had a big pink and white flower on it. Another glimpse of a whimsical side she usually hid so well.

He got to the screen door first and held it for her as they walked into the big white country kitchen.

A large old table was full of potato salad and strawberry-pretzel Jell-O and cut up vegetables. Apple pie and chocolate chip cookies. All the usual Rushford picnic favorites. Yet he had no appetite for food.

He grabbed her arm and spun her against the pantry door, then locked her in place with an arm on each side of her head. God, she was gorgeous—cheeks flushed, her hair all wild and breaking out of her ponytail. Before he could help himself, he tugged a curl and watched it spring free.

She shot him a wary look, but he could tell by her shallow breaths that she was just as affected as he was by their nearness. He looked down at her soft lips, one heartbeat away from being kissed. She closed her eyes and swallowed hard. "We're not going there again."

"I just want to talk. And I'm not touching you." He held up his hands in a gesture of surrender, but the strong desire coursed through him to kiss all the confusion out of her and replace it with pure, hot need. He'd only been touching her for seconds and his thinking was already getting muddled. He had to say what he needed to say right now.

"I admit I went to that class to be an opportunist. Because Annabelle is the only part of Kevin we have left now and I . . . guess I was ready to fight dirty to keep her here. I love that little girl as much as I loved my brother, and I'd protect her tooth and nail."

"So would I," she said.

"I came away understanding how hard you're trying to make this work. Because God knows you're giving this your all. Like you've done for everything for as long as I've known you. You're going to be a great mother to that baby. I'm sorry. For everything."

"What?" she gasped, her eyes full of surprise.

"You heard me, but so help me I'm not saying it again." He raked a hand through his hair. "Okay, dammit, I will. *I'm sorry.*"

She frowned. "Undermining me was wrong. But I understand how important family is to you."

He looked straight at her. Emotion sparked in her big brown eyes, setting off little flecks of gold and hazel he never noticed before. "I came over the other night to apologize. What happened after that just . . . happened. I wasn't trying to prey on you. It's just . . ."

"It's just . . . what?" she whispered.

They were so close he could see the tiny smattering of freckles on her nose. He wanted to kiss every one. "This connection we have is about more than just hormones, and it's time you knew it."

There. He'd said it. He saw the moment his comment registered. Watched the blush creep up her cheeks. He'd just curved his lips into a satisfied smile when she jumped up and pressed her soft pink lips to his, curled her hand around his neck and pulled him down for a kiss.

Her tongue slid around his, wet and hot, instantly torching his desire. He laced his fingers through her hair, pulled her closer and fused his lips over hers. Their tongues tangled in hungry desperation.

Every part of him wanted to mark her, claim her, this woman who smelled like citrus and berry and a hint of baby powder. Who was as familiar as his past and yet not familiar at all.

He pressed himself against her, wanted her to feel his hard, raging erection, the evidence of how crazy she made him. "God, I want you," he half whispered, half moaned as he dragged his mouth along her jaw to nip at her ear.

"Brad," she managed.

"What is it?"

"You're forgiven."

His smile curved against the soft skin of her neck. Brad lifted his head to kiss her on the mouth again when he met her gaze.

The look in her eyes stopped him cold. Trusting. Honest. True.

It reminded him of when they were eighteen and he would have done anything, anything to ensure her happiness.

God help him, he felt like that now.

But they weren't teenagers anymore. Life had grown impossibly complicated. They were different people now. Olivia was responsible for Annabelle and he had finally, after all these years, wrested free of all his child-raising responsibilities.

Olivia needed someone to stand by her, and that meant someone to father Annabelle as much as it did to love her.

He thought of all those years where he worried and fretted endlessly over his siblings. When he didn't have a clue if he was doing the right thing. How Samantha still resented him for curtailing her dreams of being an artist because he was making her get a practical degree for fear she'd end up homeless. How could he take the chance of messing up his brother's child?

He remembered the pain of breaking up with Olivia. How they couldn't seem to connect their lives. Weren't they in the same position now? How could he go through that again when his baby niece was involved?

Olivia was frowning at him. "Is something wrong?"

He opened his mouth to speak, just as a voice sounded behind them.

"I want you to stay away from my daughter."

Frank Marks stood steps away, his bushy brows knit together, his big arms crossed.

Olivia broke away, shaking a little, touching her lips with her fingers. Brad stood in front of her and faced her father. "Dad," she said, "it's all right."

"I'm sorry, honey, I can't help it," Frank said. "I overheard Alex talking to Tom. Heard she walked in on some monkey business yesterday."

Silence crackled like a hotwire. "It's not what you—" Olivia started to speak but her father continued.

"I know your type." Mr. Marks waggled a finger at Brad. "Good-looking, successful, arrogant. She doesn't need you coming around again complicating her life."

Pain stung Brad's chest. For the flash of a second, he was that hometown hick left behind, while Olivia took off for NYU.

Not good enough for her. He was never good enough in her daddy's eyes.

And never would be.

No. Brad had an MBA now, but more importantly, he was successful. He'd worked hard to educate himself and *become* something.

"Look, Mr. Marks, we've all been through a lot these last couple weeks. And maybe Olivia's been through most of all."

"Damn right. That makes my daughter vulnerable. And she doesn't need a womanizer like you trying to get in her pants."

"Dad! Please." Olivia clamped a hand on her father's arm.

Frank faced Brad nose-to-nose with his thinning hair and little pooch belly. Brad could easily take the older man down with one quick stroke.

What was he supposed to say? *I'm not trying to get in her pants,* when clearly he had been. She still held that same undeniable pull that drew him from the moment he first noticed her so long ago, sitting with her girlfriends in their usual Friday night booth at the diner.

He thought of the teenage punk who'd wanted to date his sister Samantha last year. Motorcycle, black leather kind of dude, tattooed arms. He spelled sex and Brad had practically threatened to break his arms if he so much as touched her. He'd forbidden her to see him.

But she had anyway.

He knew where Olivia's father was coming from.

"Mr. Marks, I care for your daughter. I'd never take advantage of her." She stood tight and tense, her arms crossed rigidly. Tom started to enter the kitchen, but saw what was going on and backed out quickly.

Olivia pressed between the two of them. "Are you both done discussing me? Because I'd like to say something. First, Brad, shame on you for doing *anything* to make my life more hell. But I accept your apology. And Dad, I'm almost thirty years old. I appreciate your looking out for me, but I can protect myself."

"Um, okay," Alex said, poking her head through the door. "Time to eat. Everyone grab something off that table."

"Let's go before the food gets cold," Olivia said firmly, and left to help Alex carry out the side dishes.

"I'll let this go," Frank dropped his voice so only Brad could hear. "Only because your grandmother is the most kindhearted woman in Mirror Lake, and I respect her greatly. But if I find out you've used my daughter like those other bimbos of yours, I swear I'll castrate you like a county-fair hog."

Brad stared at the older man and saw the same fury he felt fathering Samantha. "Understood."

Frank Marks was right. He wasn't good enough for his daughter. Not because he'd gone to a local university instead of a prestigious one or the fact that he'd stayed in their same small town his whole life instead of settling somewhere else more sophisticated and worldly.

Olivia needed a man willing to settle down and raise a family and he wasn't ready to commit to anybody. Most of his siblings had turned out okay in spite of all the mistakes he made, but Samantha was the wildcard and God only knew what would happen to her. And he was nowhere near ready to go through all that agony again.

Regardless of the same fierce attraction between them that made him want to rip all her clothes off and sink deep inside her sweet soft body.

It had to be doused.

Because it was just that. Attraction in the midst of a whole lot of chaos. Everything else about them was at complete odds. Their jobs, their ways of life.

And he had to keep his hands off.

CHAPTER 11

"You can't make me stay. You can't!"

Olivia froze on her porch swing, the last bottle of the day inches away from Annabelle's eagerly awaiting mouth, just as the voice of a woman hurled through Brad's open door, packed with outrage and vinegar.

What in the world? He wasn't the type to force a woman. Maybe some unusual sexual activity was going on, like role-playing? *Ew.* She started to gather her things to go back into the house, but Brad's voice from next door halted her.

"You'll do as you're told, or I'll ship your hiney right back to college." *Oh, oh.* No kinky sex games. He was speaking—okay, *yelling*—at his sister, Samantha.

"You can't do that. The dorms are closed for summer."

"Then I'll ship you to a summer camp somewhere. You can be a counselor."

"Brad, you know the plan. Buzz already has me signed up for shifts at the diner. I'm staying in town."

"Then you'll stay here."

"I'm not living in your bachelor pad. That's disgusting. And I'm not staying with Tom and Alex, either. Spike says there's plenty of room in his apartment above the auto shop garage."

"I didn't raise you to come home and parade the fact that you're moving in with some tattooed biker in front of the whole town. What will Effie say?"

"She loves me. Unlike you!"

The screen slammed, making Olivia jump. Annabelle startled. "It's okay," Olivia soothed. "Just those noisy Rushfords going at it as they're apt to do. Let's hope you got your temperament genes from *our* side of the family."

A slender young woman with an athletic build stalked across the yards and came to stand, arms crossed, on the side of Olivia's porch.

"My brother's impossible."

Olivia smiled. *Can't argue with that.*

"I'm not going back there."

"I have brownies and leftover picnic food. Come on up." Olivia did not want to entangle herself with any more problems involving Brad. God knew she was already in neck-deep. But she understood firsthand how stubborn and opinionated he could be and couldn't help but reach out.

Her visitor scaled the porch stairs in a few graceful jumps and plopped into a wicker chair. She brushed tears from her eyes and pulled a hair elastic from her wrist, twisting a dark mass of spirally curled hair on top of her head in a few quick movements.

"Samantha Rushford, all grown up and so beautiful. Come here and give me a hug."

Samantha complied, and kissed Annabelle on the forehead.

"Everything sucks so bad. My brother is riding me about *everything*. He doesn't even know I didn't start my summer class. Or that stupid research project I'm supposed to be doing. And my professors all gave me incompletes on my spring semester work and I have to retake every single one of my exams. I went back after the funeral but I-I just couldn't . . ."

Olivia reached over and squeezed her hand, doing her best not to disturb Annabelle as the baby finished her bottle and nodded off to sleep. "Oh, honey. It's okay to take some time to heal. We all need it."

"I just needed to come home, you know? But he won't even *talk* to me. When he heard me say I wanted to stay with Spike, he blew a gasket. Spike is the only one who *gets* me. He doesn't bottle up his feelings like my dumb brother does."

Olivia hesitated a second, knowing there was a fine line between kindness and interference. "You can stay here for a while. I could use a little company. If you don't mind hearing Annie cry during the night." *Brad. Was. Going. To. Kill. Her.*

On the other hand, he just might be grateful Samantha was staying with her and not Spike.

"To be honest, I'd probably sleep right through it." Samantha got up and hugged Olivia again. "Thank you. But he'll never let me."

"Let me talk with him." As if that had helped anything so far. After that embarrassing incident with her dad earlier today, he'd probably never speak to her again.

On the other hand, he did owe her big-time for that little baby class stunt he'd pulled.

"Oh, would you?" Samantha pressed her hands together in a little clap. "I'd be really grateful."

"Why don't you go in and take a shower. There are some clean T-shirts and shorts in a pile on my bed."

"A shower? But I—"

Olivia lifted Annabelle on her shoulder for a burp and stole a glance at Brad's house. "Whether you need one or not. Because here he comes now."

After Olivia deposited Annabelle in her bed, she found Brad standing outside, all lean and sexy attitude with big arms crossed and one leg propped up on the porch step. Except he looked madder than a bull with his balls tied off. And hotter than ever in a white T-shirt, shorts, and flip-flops.

The geraniums were finally taking off, thanks to her obsessive watering schedule. Realizing she hadn't done it yet today, she took her glass of iced tea from a wicker table and dumped it in one of the barrels before she sat down. Anything to delay the confrontation.

"I know she's in there," he said. "Don't deny it."

"You make it sound like I'm harboring a fugitive."

"There's a penalty for that." But he said it with a look that brought very *un*punishing images to mind. Involving lips and tongues and lots of skin-to-skin contact. Her internal temp gauge overloaded to midday Saudi Arabia instead of cool Connecticut evening, so she took a deep breath of night air to force some sense into her head. "Does it really matter if she stays here? It would give both of you a chance to calm down."

"You're meddling in my parenting skills."

She lifted a brow. "As you did with mine."

"Touché."

"In this case, somebody had to since they're clearly not working." Olivia jumped up from the swing, leaving it creaking gently as she ran into the house.

"Where are you going?" he called, irritation cutting his voice. She came out a few minutes later, carrying a sweater.

Olivia told herself she was doing this for Samantha's sake. To help everyone cool off. But breaking free from the house and all her responsibilities to spend an hour doing something fun with Brad made her positively giddy.

She wouldn't even mention the tension between him and his sister. It wasn't her business, and she shouldn't get involved.

"This way." She pushed her cell phone into the pocket of her jean capris and tugged his arm.

He stood his ground, frowning.

A slight smile escaped her lips. He was still as fiercely stubborn as a nor'easter blowing in off the coast. "There's music in the park. Plus I want ice cream. Want to come?"

"It's late."

Olivia placed her hands on her hips. "Bradley Paul Rushford, Samantha is nineteen years old and you know as well as I do that not a thing is going to be solved tonight. She has studying to do and she said she'll watch Annabelle. Now, *come on*." This time he moved—feet dragging— as she pulled him along. A little faster than a kid about to get a butt-full of shots in the doctor's office. "Fresh air will do us both some good."

"What's the band?" he asked reluctantly.

"It's a group that sings old sea chanteys and drinking songs. They do unusual stuff with a mandolin and guitar."

His expression softened microscopically, but at least he kept walking forward.

They made their way down the old tree-lined street, with sidewalks as bumpy and lopsided as crooked teeth from years of tree roots protesting against the concrete. Streetlamps lit their way past old turn-of-the-century homes, most cared for and loved, with tidy lawns and flower beds and signs of children's toys scattered in the yards, abandoned after the fine long day.

After a minute, Brad took her hand, the most simple of gestures. She looked his way, but he was surveying the neighborhood as casually as if he wasn't having a sudden heart attack and his pulse wasn't pumping off the charts like hers.

His hand was warm, his grip firm. Simple hand-holding, but it sent a thunderous wall of heat rushing through her. An unwelcome realization shook her to the core. She wanted those fine hands all over her body, roaming, exploring, making her moan.

"Um," she said, lifting up their joined hands.

A wicked sparkle flashed in his eyes. God, he was sexy and danger-ous-looking when angry but gorgeous beyond words when he smiled.

Maybe this was a bad idea. She wasn't sure how much longer she could resist him.

"Um, what?" he asked innocently.

"Um, I wasn't sure you'd be talking to me after the picnic?"

He chuckled, a warm sound that soothed her agitated insides. "Your dad is just looking out for you. I'd feel the same way about Samantha. But I didn't think you'd be talking to me, either."

"Why not?"

He stopped walking and pinned her with his dark, intense gaze. A gaze that made her go gooey as melted caramel on the inside. "You know. After the way I tried to undermine you."

He could undermine her any time he liked if he looked at her like that, as if he was about to lick her like an ice cream cone and devour her in one bite.

"I've been thinking you're right about one thing. I have to figure out how to change my life for Annabelle's benefit. I asked my boss if I could reduce my hours and do more work from home."

"When do you hear back?" Did he sound hopeful? Pleased? Why did she care?

"She's working on it. Any day now."

"That's great. I'm sure you'll make it work, no matter what happens."

They continued on in silence as the quaint residential neighbor-hood gave way to larger, older homes that once belonged to town founders and mayors and even a Gilded Age shipping baron or two. One had been converted into the B and B, which glowed with wel-coming lights and overflowing flower baskets. Brad paused to chat with a young couple pushing a stroller and walking with two tod-dlers carrying raspberry-red balloons, out enjoying the perfect spring evening.

"I've forgotten how friendly everyone is," Olivia said as they moved on to downtown.

Brad shrugged. "It's who we are. Suppose that's what happens when everybody knows everybody."

"It's different with my neighbors in New York. Mrs. Bertolini occasionally says 'hi' when forced, and the reclusive author down the hall comes out once or twice a year for air and groceries." People were more unguarded here, and that was nice. Before she could get sentimental about it, Olivia reminded herself how quickly that quality could veer into buttinsky range.

They walked in silence for a while, passing Pie in the Sky and Mona's. Across the street, in the park, a crowd gathered around the gazebo and the strains of a fiddle and mandolin drifted toward them. Call her crazy, but she decided to bite the bullet. For Samantha's sake. "Funny that both of us were suddenly thrust into parenthood."

Brad smiled. "With intensive on-the-job training."

"You've done a great job with your siblings."

"The boys I handled, somehow. It's the girl who's the thorn in my side."

"I remember when she was around eight, you were her champion. You taught her how to stand up to that mean girl who kept stealing her lunch."

He laughed. "We packed two lunches and she hid one in her book bag. The bologna sandwich she put in plain view in her locker had hot sauce on it. That solved the problem pretty quickly."

"And remember how you tossed her a softball over and over until she learned to catch so she wouldn't be the last one to be picked for a team?"

"Yeah, well, the issues are more complicated now. I'm not her hero any longer."

"You might be surprised." He looked unconvinced. "She'll be all right. You both will be." She touched his arm to second that. When he slowed his pace and glanced at her, struggle and worry shadowed his eyes. Why would he feel so much pain about a child who was kind-hearted and good and clearly not a failure in any sense of the word?

"She does things just to get under my skin. And she thinks she's in love with some deadbeat punk with a jewel in his nose. Who will use her then dump her. And I won't have my sister taken advantage of like that."

"It's called a nose piercing. And she wouldn't be home if she didn't love you. She's just hurting, like all of us."

"It didn't start with Kevin's death. Samantha has always been the one who's been the best at pushing the splinter further under my thumb. First it was skipping classes to protest animal cruelty. Then it was taking off on a whim to drive cross-country with a friend because she wanted to see the Grand Canyon. She wanted to take a year off before college and I wouldn't let her. Now she's talking about art school. *Art* school. What kind of job is she going to get from that?"

"Artists can do quite well. I have a friend—"

"Don't, Olivia." Brad blew out a frustrated breath. "I've heard it all. The point is, I'm responsible for her until she's an adult. I have to make sure she turns out okay. And so far I've failed miserably. I begged her to study for the SAT. Do you know what she did? Got an extra job just to spite me—so she could say she had no time to study."

Olivia grabbed his elbow and pulled until he came to a stop. She'd meant it as a grab-your-attention gesture but her fingertips tingled at the contact with his warm skin. He was a fiercely protective man who deeply loved his family. And that was wildly appealing.

"Brad. Stop beating yourself up. Cut Samantha some slack."

"She's doing it to spite me."

Olivia tossed up her hands. "Why on earth would she want to spite you? Except for the fact she's a teenager and that's what they do."

He shifted his weight. He wore khaki walking shorts and his calves were toned and lean and so distracting. Suddenly he was far more appealing than ice cream.

"Because I screwed up. She's always known how to test me, push all the buttons. Out of fear, I tried to squash her rebelliousness. And I was too harsh. It only made her want to rebel more. I'm not cut out for parenting, plain and simple."

He screwed up? Mr. Take Charge of Everything? If she didn't see the tense set of his shoulders and the agonized expression in his eyes, she never would have believed it. Every impulse in her wanted to gather him close and comfort him, but he was a proud man, and she'd never seen him admit weakness like this. "You were so young when you had to take charge," she said quietly. "You did the best you could."

"I didn't have a clue what I was doing. And with Samantha, it shows."

"You're afraid she's going to get in trouble. Sleep with the nose-piercing guy, get pregnant, stop school, that kind of thing?" He gave a terse nod. "It's the same thing my dad worried about with me and you. In fact, he's still worried, if what he said at the picnic is any indication."

"I worked my ass off and I'm successful. It's a little different."

"In his mind, you still had sex with me, and that's all that counts."

"It was a lot more than that, Liv." His brutally intense gaze drilled into her, making goose bumps rise like tiny pinpricks all over her arms.

Oh, yeah, it was. And maybe it still is. But by then they were in the middle of downtown, in front of the Dairy Flip. The big window showed a long counter with bright pink stools and a sign that said *Flavor of the day: strawberry chocolate cheesecake,* but the lights were dim and no one was inside. "They're closed," Olivia said. She'd invented the ice cream reason to get him away from Samantha but now she was actually disappointed.

"We must've just missed it." Brad checked his Rolex. "You still up for ice cream?"

Olivia rolled her eyes. "*Hello.* When am I *not* up for ice cream?"

"Come with me."

He grabbed her hand and pulled her along Main Street, under the glow of the old-fashioned post lights. They cut through the park, where a four-person band was packing up and people were dispersing.

"Looks like we missed the ice cream *and* the dancing," Olivia said.

"Not necessarily."

They walked another block to the marina, where Reflections sat basking near the water in a glow of subdued landscape lighting.

"I want to show you my restaurant." His eyes held a look of eager excitement, like a boy about to tear open a birthday present. She was thrilled beyond words that he'd brought her here. "If you want to see it, of course."

"I'd love to." She remembered the night she'd come here with Alex, how Brad had come over to advise them about the menu. It had felt wrong, both of them being there with other people. She felt his pride now, understood how important this was to him after all his years of scraping and saving.

Inside, she caught glimpses of polished wood, crisp white table-cloths, flickering candles. A wonderful mix of aromas—seafood, garlic, butter, and rich coffee—filled the air. A few couples lingered at the bar at this late hour, talking quietly as soft jazz played over the speakers. Brad introduced her to his kitchen staff and headed directly over to a huge walk-in freezer. "Wait here," he said, disappearing inside.

A minute later he reappeared. "We have vanilla rosemary, chocolate graham cracker, and lemon frozen yogurt." He looked at her expectantly. "The chocolate it is."

"I didn't say which flavor yet."

"You don't have to. Your eyes glazed over when I said 'chocolate.'"

They took their ice cream outside and sat on the dock with their feet dangling over the water, close to the still roped-off deck. Lights from lakeside businesses reflected off the water, and across the lake, a lighthouse beam intermittently scanned the sky. The same soft jazz piped outside over the speakers.

"Is it as good as Dairy Flip?" Olivia asked, looking down at her ice cream. "I mean, with the fancy flavors and all, I wasn't sure."

"Don't judge my ice cream till you've tried it."

Olivia dug in. It wasn't long before she'd scraped her bowl and licked the spoon, setting it down with a *chink*. "Amazing," she said on a sigh.

"You always did have a thing for ice cream." One second he was chuckling and the next he was extending his arm, pulling her up and walking with her onto the newly built deck.

"What are you doing?" she asked on a sudden breath, her hands pushing against the hard muscles of his broad chest as she tried to find balance.

"I thought since we missed dancing, we could do it here." Brad swept her into his arms and did a few turns, the fresh sawdust *scricking* under their shoes. He led with grace, panache, and the confidence of a man used to sweeping a hell of a lot of females off their feet.

The moon was as large as a full scoop of vanilla, casting glistening, pearly caps on the waves. The smell of the lake was familiar and soothing, but the feel of Brad's muscles flexing under her fingertips was dangerous and unsettling.

As the song ended, he took a final turn and dipped her low.

He pulled her up slowly, inching her closer to his magnificent body. At last she was upright, staring into the depths of his warm, green eyes. Eyes that looked straight into her and told her he wanted her six ways to Sunday right now.

Her mouth went dry, and her thoughts tumbled aimlessly, unable to form into words. Oh, she was in big trouble.

"I remember the last time I saw you on a dance floor," he said.

"Trish and Kevin's wedding. You came with a gorgeous model with a wildly inappropriate dress and legs as long as I-95."

"You were with that Wall Street guy with the thousand-dollar suit."

"You tongued her on the dance floor."

"When I found out you were engaged to him. What happened with that, anyway?"

She shrugged. "He wasn't the type to eat ice cream on a dock or dance on a bunch of sawdust in the moonlight."

Oh, God, she shouldn't have said that. Too revealing.

"I'm glad you didn't marry him."

His words hung still as the sand-dollar moon glistening over the water. They stopped moving. The earth stood still. The piped-out music faded to black. All she saw was Brad's beautiful face, his soft, kind eyes, green as the sea. She melted under his sizzling gaze, her knees caving. She had to remind herself to drag air into her chest, as though she forgot how to breathe.

Just like so long ago.

And God, she wanted him, a hundred times more than back then, when she knew nothing about life or love. She would never fit as perfectly with anyone.

But he didn't want forever, especially forever with a child. That was even clearer after what he'd just said about his sister. And she owed Annabelle more than a man who could only promise a one-night stand. She forced herself to pull back.

"Brad, I don't think—"

"Why'd we break up, anyway?" he interrupted. He was still so close. Everything about him overwhelmed, his just-showered scent, the sudden brutal honesty of his gaze.

The question caught her off-balance. "Well, from what I recall, we both changed after I left. I think it was your classic case of going away and growing apart."

He grabbed her by the arms. "That's the polite version. I want to know what you really thought."

She sighed and closed her eyes, unwilling to dredge up painful memories. "Okay, you want the truth, then here it goes. That first semester away, I was excited about everything. Maybe too excited. I'd probably gone on and on about the people I'd met, the places I'd seen. You must have thought I was spoiled, going to parties and having fun while you were working your ass off."

"I had no concept of the things you talked about at college. I was afraid when you came home at Christmas that you saw me as little more than a country boy."

"I never thought of you like that."

"I couldn't compete with your new life. You'd changed and I hadn't. I didn't think you'd even really missed me."

"I missed you desperately. But when you came to visit, nothing went well. You hated my friends. We couldn't communicate anymore."

"I expect I was resentful. Pitied myself, thought I wasn't good enough."

"I thought you didn't care enough about me to make it work." Olivia squeezed her eyes shut. She remembered the devastation. The hurt, the anger. Their differences had seemed permanent, like visible scars that would never go away.

She'd told herself it was just as well, that she could never see herself settling in Mirror Lake, on the same scary path as her mother, tied down by marriage and kids and unable to accomplish what she needed to make her happy.

"I knew I would only hold you back. Drag you down. Bring you back to a place you outgrew." He cupped her face with his hand, smoothed his thumb over her cheek. She was mesmerized by the rough feel paired with the most gentle of motions. "Letting you go was the worst mistake I ever made."

Oh, what she wouldn't have given to hear that through all those lonely years, when no one she dated had ever matched up to him.

"In some ways I did think of myself as more sophisticated, more worldly. I guess we both had a lot of maturing to do."

"Seeing your success spurred me to go to college, then to grad school. I knew there was more out there. I wanted to better myself."

"You've done really well."

"I own a yacht. It's docked a ways down the marina. I've traveled all over Europe, and I own a place in Key West where I can get away in winter."

He looked a little sad. Why was he telling her this?

"I don't really take much time off," she said.

His lips tipped up in a half smile. "You only get one life. Work hard, play hard, that's my motto."

The magazine spread with Brad flanked by the Greek beauties flashed in her mind. Yes, he played hard. Instinctively, she backed up a step.

She didn't know anything but work. Had always been hell-bent on accomplishing something, being something. Proving to everyone she was somebody other than a throw-away child, a kid not good enough or perfect enough to get her own mother to stay.

Maybe she'd spend the rest of her life using work to fill the void her mother's lack of love had left.

Against her will, tears stung her eyes. She turned away, toward the lake, pretending to be engrossed by the view.

Brad came up behind her and held her. "You'll be a fine mother to Annabelle. You'll find balance."

She felt the secure weight of his hands on her upper arms. Every part of her yearned to lean back into his solid chest and let his strong arms surround her. Stay forever in his secure embrace. But the weight of the burden she carried was too heavy.

Olivia turned to face Brad. She had to let out the terrible fear she hadn't admitted to anyone. "I'll do anything to be worthy to be her mother. I look at Annabelle and I don't understand how anyone could ever leave a child. Like my mother did. But I'll never understand why Trish picked me."

"You're her sister. She loved you."

"Maybe it was an accident. You don't think much about dying when you're young. She was in a rush to get that will done before she had Annabelle. And she had to put *somebody* down . . ."

Brad brushed a wisp of her hair aside. His touch was as gentle as his voice. "Did you ever think that maybe she wanted Annabelle to grow up to be like you—strong and independent?"

"But I can't do what she would really want, to keep Annabelle here with her family. I'm not like everyone here. My DNA's not a part of this town."

"You're not your mother, Olivia."

She blinked. How did he sense her deepest fear?

"Your mom was restless and bored here. But she didn't have your education, your resources. The world is all connected now."

"There aren't exactly any jobs in my field here. And the pace of life is certainly different. I mean, the newspaper doesn't even show up at Gertie's before noon."

A double line creased his forehead. "I was a fool for letting you go the way I did, but I was young and stupid and I'm sorry for it. But honestly, what you're saying"—he tapped his index finger on her chest— "It's all a big excuse."

"What?" Irritation sparked inside her like a match. Who was he to judge her?

He seemed angry now, pacing in front of her. She didn't think she'd insulted the town, but he loved it so much, maybe she'd struck a nerve. "Don't hide behind the excuse of our town being small. Maybe you can't consider any alternatives for your life because you're afraid of who you are without your job."

She tapped her own chest emphatically. "I don't make excuses. I *act*. My whole life has been about attacking a goal and doing everything possible to succeed."

"Maybe at work, but not in your personal life. You've forgotten what success really is. You think it's your job and your big-city life, but what have you really got? Do you ever have any fun? Your best friends never see you, and your father tells me you work all the time. Is that a successful life?"

Her guts twisted in her belly like a wet rag. Tears burned but she'd never give him the satisfaction of seeing them.

Oh, God. How could she possibly explain that she had no idea who she was without her work? No one. She would be no one. Work had saved her. Given her a sense of importance. Offered her an opportunity to lose herself in something greater and all-encompassing so she'd never be that throw-away child again.

Even if she agreed to stay here in Mirror Lake, how would she prevent herself from becoming restless and bored? And over time, as bitter and resentful as her own mother. She liked to think she was nothing like her, but what if she was? Her mother was a bright, high-achieving woman. And this town had destroyed her.

"How dare you judge me!" she lashed out. "Sure, you have your restaurants and your boats and your vacation houses. And any woman you could want. You'd do anything to keep yourself unattached and uncommitted, but what good is all that freedom, Brad? You wouldn't know what a real relationship was if"—she fumbled around for a clever phrase but nothing came—"if Darcy and Elizabeth were your BFFs." Lame, that the only example of a happy couple she could pluck from the air was two hundred years old. And fictional. No matter, she'd spilled all her ire, just as he had. It was all out there now, never to be taken back.

She'd lashed out at him because he'd hurt her. And, if she were completely honest, because he'd put his hand directly on her Achilles' heel and pressed hard.

His brows lowered over a narrowed gaze. "You have no business criticizing my right to freedom after all those years I spent without it."

"Well, you can have it. In fact, you can take your freedom and stick it!"

She strode off, away from him, back toward the road leading to the square. His angry steps clattered on the deck behind her.

He swung her around to face him, his eyes lit with fury.

"You're right, Olivia. You are driven, and who am I to ask you to reverse the tide, go backward to everything you hate. You know your place, and I know mine. Guess we're on the same page after all."

The ice cream lurched in her stomach. The perfect moonlit evening was ruined with a few bitter words. What had started out so magical had blown up into their worst fight ever. "Then I guess I'd better head back home."

She did not miss the irony that they were fighting the same fight they should have had years ago, but like then, through life, circumstances, or bone-deep stubbornness, there would be no resolution.

She walked off, leaving him standing alone on his brand new deck.

CHAPTER 12

The next morning, Brad got out of his Popsicle-red Audi R8 Coupe and crunched over Olivia's gravel drive. He couldn't concentrate at work. She plagued his fantasies, his dreams, and every waking moment. She made him furious, but still all he could think of was pushing her into the nearest wall and doing all sorts of very interesting things to her until they were both sweaty and exhausted and there was nothing left to fight about.

He knew—*knew* just as certainly as he knew his own birthday—despite all their differences, making love would be the one language they'd both speak fluently. Where they'd be in perfect sync. Too bad that came with all sorts of complications two stubborn people like them couldn't seem to get around.

Brad checked his phone, scrolling over a list of missed calls and messages then thrusting the damn thing in his pocket. Irritation pricked at him. He had out-of-town business for the next two days and Olivia's time here was ticking down. He had to take action now.

As soon as he stepped onto the porch, an alarming whine assailed his ears. The obnoxious chirping of a smoke detector. Fear squeezed adrenaline through his veins. He rattled the handle of the old wood door. *Locked.* Besides Olivia's car in the driveway, Annabelle's stroller sat on the porch. His heart stopped, sudden as a thunderclap, in his chest.

He tried kicking in the door but it wouldn't budge. The kitchen window was open, so he used the penknife on his key chain to slit the screen and climb through. No smoke in the kitchen, but a sharp, acrid odor and the high-pitched pulse of the alarm, ten times louder than it was from outside. It was coming from the hallway. A thin trace of smoke snaked from the first floor bathroom. He called out Olivia's name as he followed the stinging smell.

No answer.

A curling iron sat propped on the edge of the bathroom sink, its red light glowing, the hot metal roller touching the side of a plastic tissue box—and melting it. Brad pulled the plug, pushed the iron into the sink, and threw open the bathroom window.

As he ran back into the kitchen, he stopped in his tracks. Olivia stood in the middle of the room in a pink terry bathrobe, a shocked look on her face, her hair dripping.

Two emotions hit him at once. *Thank God she's alive* and *Lord, she is gorgeous.*

"What is it?" Panic filled her voice.

"Curling iron." His voice was surprisingly shaky. "I unplugged it."

"Oh, thank God." She dragged a kitchen chair to the hallway, centered it under the smoke alarm, and stood on it, her hands pulling her belt taut around her waist.

Gulp.

His ears were exploding from the noise but he barely noticed it with the sight of her, wet, luscious, and dripping, straining to reach the ceiling with one hand while trying to keep the flaps of her robe together with the other.

He'd like to help her with that problem, but he wasn't sure she'd like his solution.

The robe shifted upward, revealing miles of soft, shapely thighs directly at eye level. The scents of simple Dove soap and berry shampoo surrounded him like a cloud.

Seconds ticked. Brad stood there for untold moments staring at the shaded border between skin and robe, as she fumbled with the smoke detector.

He'd criticized Olivia for being afraid to stay but he never once said he *wanted* her to stay. He liked being in control, and not getting attached meant total control and zero heartache from being left behind again.

Except all he could think of is what had just happened. What if he hadn't come by, and Olivia had stayed obliviously in her shower until the entire house had gone up in flames?

What if he'd lost her, the only woman who'd ever meant anything to him? What if their story had ended before it even began, deadlocked by their own stubbornness?

He shook off the terrible thought and swallowed hard.

Sudden silence jarred his brain.

"Finally." Olivia held the nine-volt battery in her hand.

Their gazes locked. The old clock ticked away moments heavy with indecision. Common sense told him *no*. A million years of evolution cried *absolutely yes*.

Olivia gave a little gasp. She always read his thoughts better than anybody. Her hand reached up instinctively to pull her robe lapels closer. "I must have forgotten to turn the curling iron off."

"Nice try but your hair's sopping wet. I know it was Samantha's."

"Brad, she's been going through a lot lately. Please don't add this to everything else."

"Leaving a curling iron on is irresponsible. If something would have happened . . ." Horrifying images passed in front of his eyes. He squeezed his eyes shut to make them stop.

Olivia shook his shoulders. "It was an accident. Annabelle was fussing and Samantha was in a hurry to be on time for her first day. And the smoke detector did its job."

She was so passionate about it. He couldn't help but be touched about her concern for his sister. "I'll take that into consideration. Like you said—maybe I can cut her some slack. We've all been through a lot."

"Oh." She sounded surprised that he gave in a little. Frankly, he wasn't thinking about Samantha right now. At all.

Olivia stood on tiptoe on the chair to snap the smoke detector lid shut, giving Brad the opportunity to notice that her legs ran for miles, tanned and toned. His fingers itched to feel their silky texture, so close and tempting. Her tanned skin stood out over the pale pink of the robe. He wondered where the tan would stop.

Brad held out a hand to help her down from the chair, working hard to focus on her eyes and not the little peek of cleavage visible under her robe. As she took his hand, they both froze. His mind stuttered. "Olivia I-I came over here today because I can't stop thinking about you. If anything would have happened to you or the baby . . ." His voice cracked on the last word as emotion overcame him and he let it all out.

"I could have lost you without ever telling you how special you are to me. That same magic I felt when I was eighteen—I feel it now, and I've never felt it with anyone but you. I eat, sleep, and dream about you and I want you more than I've ever wanted anyone else, period."

She gasped.

He grabbed her and lowered her slowly, enjoying the contact of her hips, her breasts, as he released her slowly down his body until she stood on the floor. Those big eyes of hers softened with desire, and he knew she wanted him, too. For a flash, he wondered what it would be like with all the barriers down between them. With nothing holding them back.

As he held her in his arms, a sense of complete and swift relief engulfed him to the point of near panic. He sucked at expressing his feelings. Hated not being in control. Hated that whatever he said would *matter* because Olivia mattered. She could have been lost to him, like Kevin and Trish. Suddenly all their problems dimmed in comparison.

She touched his cheek, and he slid his own hand up to cover hers. In that electrifying second, all the pain and confusion that had passed in the last few weeks rose up in his chest and he heaved a deep breath.

She understood. Her other hand reached up and smoothed the rough stubble on his face. Caressed him.

"I want you to stay," he whispered. "More than I want to breathe."

Her touch calmed him. Mesmerized him. "You were right about me, Brad. That's why I lashed out at you. I'm afraid of who I am without my job. Of becoming my mother, discontented and unhappy in the suburbs."

"Quit trying to please her. She left you. That was her problem, not yours. You're a lot stronger than she was."

She nodded, as if trying to believe that. He stood there frozen, transfixed by the gentle feel of her hand against his skin.

He rested his forehead against hers. Inhaled her clean fragrance, basked in her warmth. The restless clock ticked away precious seconds. Her arms wrapped around his neck and locked tight.

Brad had comforted everyone, but no one had held him since Kevin died. That simple pleasure affected him beyond words. Everything about Olivia was sweet and so, so addictive—the gentleness of her smile, the softness of her touch, but most of all, the fact that she got him when no one else did.

He curled his fingers around the nape of her neck and kissed her.

The worst possible kind of kiss, so different from the other night, when it was all about lust.

This one was about need, the deep, uncontrollable kind. Far over and above the sexual kind and more about the frightening, endless kind he feared more than anything.

"I-I can't think," Olivia said.

"Don't." He wasn't demanding, he was begging. In that moment, he couldn't bear her to leave. He needed her. Maybe he always had.

He pulled her to him till her breasts pressed softly into his chest, well aware there was only a damp robe holding him back from her luscious curves.

He planted his mouth over hers in a move of absolute possession. There would be no thinking. Lips ground together, tongues collided as he branded her for his own. Stroke for stroke, she met him and demanded as much as she gave.

He was greedy for all of her, as if his great need could make up for the many years they'd missed. His hands traced the damp skin of her neck just below the robe and tangled in her wet hair.

The robe parted. A flash of toned leg appeared. He took advantage of the opportunity to slide his hand up her outer thigh and hover there.

He caressed her inner thigh, teasing her, while he pushed the robe aside and rained kisses down her neck and shoulder. Her cool hands roved over his chest, skimmed his back and butt, holding him in an electrifying trance as she explored everywhere.

He remembered how it was a long time ago. Needy and frantic and desperate. *Just like this.*

He pulled the robe down with his teeth until he freed her beautiful breast and took the rosy tip into his mouth, encasing it in the warmth and wetness of his mouth. A whimper tore from her throat.

He pulled his mouth away and looked up at her. "Is this what you want?" He had to hear it from her lips, her choice.

She grabbed his face, looked directly into his eyes. He'd never seen such a clear, honest gaze, like she was looking directly into his soul, and it made his own heart crack open with joy. "I want you."

With a single flicking movement of her hands, the robe dropped, exposing the sweetest curves he'd ever seen. Awe swept through him, as if he were seeing her for the first time.

"You're more beautiful now than before." He touched her shoulder reverently, as if she were a shrine he'd journeyed miles to worship at. Traced down the smooth curve of her collarbone. She stood there unselfconsciously, as mesmerized by his touch as he was by hers.

In a quick move, he sat on the chair and dragged her over so she straddled his legs. Her curves were exquisite, so soft, draped like a luscious curtain all over him. Their kisses grew more and more fevered, her muscles tensing and her bottom squirming as he held her tight against him.

Dimly, a distant wail cut into his consciousness. Except he was lost, far gone in the sweet taste of her, in the soft moans that emanated deep in her throat, in the velvet feel of her soft flesh tensing against his hand.

Until it became louder. At first he thought it was the baby, but no—sirens sounded up close now, slashing through their dream world, imposing an ear-splitting reality check.

Olivia broke their kiss abruptly, her lips pulling away with a soft smack. She jumped out of his arms and reached for her discarded robe.

"Shit," he said.

On the kitchen counter, the baby monitor lit up, one red warning light at a time until a whole row strobed back and forth before them.

Annabelle let out a discontented wail. His first impulse was to do the same.

The baby's cries heightened in pitch and intensity.

Brad's whole body was humming. He reached for Olivia one last time, held her tight while he tried to slow his racing heart and take in some air.

Reality flooded back into her eyes, replacing the starry-eyed gaze that made him so crazy. She held her hands against his chest and pushed weakly. "I have to go before the entire fire department walks in."

Flushed, her hair hanging in wet spirals, she was the most beautiful woman he'd ever seen.

She kissed him on the forehead. A sweet kiss, in stark contrast to the hot, wet kisses from moments ago, but it made his gut clench uncomfortably.

She stirred him too deeply, in an unforgiving way that pulled his heart from his chest and twisted it so it would never fit back in. She broke all his boundaries, left him naked in more ways than one, and he didn't like it at all.

"I have to get the baby," she said softly.

"I'll field the fire department."

"I'm . . . glad you stopped by," she said, grinning. "To talk, that is."

He grinned back. "I'd say we got a lot accomplished."

She got him like no one else ever had, and that scared the shit out of him. He'd had lots of women, but this had been different. Way different. He didn't want to feel it, didn't want to want her because he knew too well what it would be like when she was gone. And if he knew one thing for sure, she *would* go.

But when he'd barged into that house, and smelled that burning scent, and feared the worst . . . well, it had scared him big-time.

Engines cut off. Sirens silenced. Truck doors slammed. Out the window, a handful of EMS guys marched up to the back door.

"Olivia," Brad called.

She turned. "Yes?"

"Just to let you know—this fire's not out yet."

Her eyes twinkled. "I'd say it's only just getting started."

She headed for the stairs. He opened the door for the fire crew, smiling a little too widely.

CHAPTER 13

"I'm on edge waiting for my boss to call to discuss the new schedule I proposed." Olivia lifted her gaze to her two oldest and dearest friends, who sat across from her at the ancient orange Formica-topped table at the front of Pie in the Sky. She traced the circular grooves on her coffee mug then tapped it fretfully. Agitation knotted her stomach and the smells of diner food—burgers, fries, mashed potatoes and gravy—made it worse. "And the house still smells like burnt plastic even though it's been three days."

Meg and Alex exchanged knowing glances. They weren't buying her explanations for why she seemed to be in such a funk. Meg put down her tea and sat back in the old booth. "Just tell us what's up with Brad. We know he's what's bothering you, so out with it already."

Olivia opened her mouth to speak but thoughts of her pink bathrobe and the smoke alarm and Brad's hands roving all over her body made her choke back the words.

"Sexual frustration, that's my diagnosis. Am I right?" Alex watched her pointedly. Saw the moment when heat flooded Olivia's cheeks, and she was all over it. "Bingo! The cure is to sleep with him already."

The elderly couple in the booth across glanced over and frowned. Even Buzz, the owner, looked up from the grill behind the counter.

"Alex, will you shush?" Meg's usual soft voice was edged with irritation. Olivia felt comfort in their banter, so familiar after all the times they'd spent in this very booth near the big plate-glass window that overlooked the square. In the late Friday afternoon sunshine, there was some commotion happening outside, with trucks and trailers crowding the street next to the grassy park.

Alex pointed an accusatory finger at Meg. "You're the one who bet me five bucks they already did it." Her gaze shifted to Olivia. "So why didn't you? Sleep with him, that is."

Olivia reached in the booth next to her to retuck the blanket Annabelle had just kicked off. It was a little chilly with the air conditioning. Annabelle found the corner of the blanket and began to suck on it.

"You're the one who broke it up between us, as I recall," Olivia said.

"That was when I thought he was using you. Before I saw all that smoking-hot combustion between you two. So what happened?"

"We almost did it. But Brad's gone on business and I've had time to come to my senses. He's made it clear he's not looking for a long-term relationship. I have to think of what's best for Annabelle." The past few days had allowed her to reason this out. A fling was definitely not what was best.

No matter how desperately she wanted him.

And it would be a fling, with a man who might want her to stay but who feared commitment and raising another child. And let's face it, she couldn't give up the security of her job even if she could find freelance projects that might allow her to work remotely. Not as a single mother with a child to raise and put through college.

Yes, it was good the fire department had shown up. Good he was out of town. Because she didn't want to start a dead-end romance. She'd gotten over him once, but it had taken years. She couldn't put herself through that again.

If she expected sympathy to gush from her friends' mouths, she didn't get it.

Alex's mug hit the Formica with a thud. "Olivia, what do you expect the man to do? You're leaving for New York. Just like ten years ago. You can't blame him for being gun-shy."

No, she couldn't. But he wanted his freedom and she had a one-month-old.

"Maybe you should talk with him. Have a heart-to-heart," Meg said.

Yeah, right. Except every time they started that, they ended up peeling off each other's clothes. Or arguing. Mostly both.

"But all that chemistry—it practically explodes," Meg said.

"I saw how Brad looked at you at the picnic the other day," Alex said. "Like you were dessert. A s'more. And he wanted some. More."

As Alex chuckled at her own joke, Olivia shook her head. "There will always be this crazy hormone thing between us. But that doesn't mean we have to act on it. That could get very messy."

"Life is messy," Alex said firmly. "And you've still got your pressed Sunday dress on with a clean hem."

Alex's words struck home. Her friend was accusing her of holding back on living her life just like Brad had.

Buzz approached with a fresh pot of coffee. Alex immediately held out her mug for a refill.

Buzz bent his stocky frame toward Annabelle and waggled his fingers. "Coochie coochie coo." Annabelle kicked her feet like a bongo drummer in response. The blanket fell to the floor. "She's one adorable baby. Anyone else want a topper?"

Olivia nodded. "Thanks, Buzz." As he poured the coffee, she said, "You haven't changed one bit."

He patted his stomach under his white apron. "I think I put on a few sympathy pounds with Cheryl being pregnant." He paused awkwardly. "I just want to say I admire you for what you've done, Olivia, coming back here from that big city job of yours . . ."

In the past week, so many townspeople had expressed their sympathy. That awkward stab of pain was back. Actually, it never really left, but this time Olivia decided to deal with it and place the focus on what really mattered: Annabelle. Trish would want that.

She flashed Buzz a big smile. "This baby is a wonder. Look what she does." She leaned down to speak to the baby, and while she was at it, retrieve the blanket. "Let's show everyone what you just learned, honey. Show them you're the sweetest baby that ever lived."

The baby flashed a gummy smile that showed off two of her chins. Then she stuck her foot in her mouth. Olivia gently pulled it out and looked around the table proudly. "That's her latest accomplishment."

"That's pretty acrobatic," Buzz said.

Meg *tsked.* "Buzz, she just smiled. Isn't she *amazing*?"

So many times over the past few days, Olivia had wanted to run across the yard and drag Brad back to show him, forgetting he wasn't there.

Alex took a peek. "Usually I don't think babies are cute, but she's adorable."

"Smart, too," Meg added.

Olivia frowned. "Alex, you couldn't possibly think your own babies weren't cute."

"Oh, yes I could. Not a one was the least bit cute until they started sleeping through the night. Honestly, I was so sleep deprived, I don't even remember what they looked like."

Olivia smiled at her friends. What would she do without Alex's snarkiness and Meg's loyalty? Or the friendship that had cheered and comforted her through all kinds of tribulations? It was like she'd never left. She'd missed them, and it made her sad these times together would be ending soon.

Maybe Brad was right. In her scramble for success, her priorities had gotten pushed out of place. "I just wanted to tell you two how much I appreciate how you've been there for me. I'd never survive this without you and . . . well, I love you both so much." She grasped their hands across the table.

"We love you, too, Olivia," Meg said, squeezing her hand.

"And we want you to be happy," Alex added.

"Okay, I love you all, too, but I'm going back to the kitchen." Buzz fled the table as quickly as possible.

"We love you, too, Buzz," Meg called as Buzz waved them off. Then she turned back to the table. "Olivia's right. She's going back to New York next week. And she'll have to face Brad whenever she comes back to visit. That could be really awkward."

"She's already slept with him back in high school. This would be for old times' sake." Alex sipped her coffee. "You know, Olivia, I was always surprised you did that. Of all of us, you always went by the book. You studied, ate your veggies, and didn't push your curfew. How on earth did you end up having sex with Brad?"

Easy answer. He was irresistible. "We were young and foolish. I'm not foolish anymore." She placed a hand over her chest for emphasis. "I know in my heart it would be ridiculous to get involved now." Olivia felt her heartbeat, strong and rebellious under her hand. It didn't seem to care that she had a job and a life in New York and that Brad's life was as entwined around Mirror Lake as ivy climbing bricks.

Meg, probably sensing her confusion, rested a hand on her arm. "I always thought you two would marry."

Olivia blinked in surprise. Meg often based her own decisions on emotion and intuition. In Meg's case, that meant she chose guys who were needy and intense, who required being taken care of.

"I don't think Brad's ever really gotten over you," Meg said.

Olivia flicked her hand. "Oh, please."

"Then how come he's never found *the one* either?"

Had she ever felt that magic, that karma since? It was crazy to believe she'd found it the very first time she'd fallen in love with a man. "Brad doesn't believe in the magic of love. He thinks marriage is all about responsibility and paying bills and screwing up your kids."

"Logic never works," Meg said. "It's all about passion."

"Meg, I swear. You talk the big talk but you do nothing to get Benjamin Rushford to notice you."

Meg fidgeted with her spoon. "We live in a town the size of a dime. If he wanted me, he would have noticed me by now."

"There's nothing wrong with giving a man a little nudge, honey." Alex sat back and crossed her arms. "That goes for both of you. Olivia, your time's flying by. What are you going to do?"

"Be neighborly, be polite. I'll be back in New York in a week."

Alex narrowed her eyes, never being one for bullshit. "Last chance for a future with Brad."

Anxiety churned the strong coffee in Olivia's stomach. The puzzle pieces were locked in. She had to keep her job. He had to stay here, in the town he loved, where he was successful, popular, and happy. Changing anything would be like moving Sisyphus's boulder. *Impossible.*

Meg sighed. "I hate to see you go. You don't come home enough."

Olivia patted Meg's hand. "You'll just have to come to New York. We'll have a girls' weekend."

Alex frowned. "That's a little hard when you work seven days a week. So when will you hear back from that boss of yours?"

"Any time now. If I can just scale back a bit, I just might be able to do this. I've been Skyping with nanny candidates and have it narrowed down to two. And I was hoping to maybe work Fridays from home."

Olivia glanced down at the baby. Annabelle had not only kicked the blanket off but also both socks and somehow had one in her mouth. Olivia pulled the sock from her mouth and kissed her foot on the way down to pick up the other stuff.

"Speaking of Brad," Meg said, pointing out the window. "There he is."

Olivia jerked her eyes across the street. The trucks had pulled away, exposing the walkways and benches and white gazebo with curlicue trim, now draped with garlands of white flowers.

"They must be setting up for a wedding," Alex said.

"Nope," Meg said. "Prom tonight."

But the square was only a distraction. Brad stood in the front yard of the old red brick Victorian with a woman in a business suit, talking animatedly and pointing up at the roof.

Ancient, buried feelings rushed back as Olivia stared at the regal Queen Anne with its sprawling covered porch and a majestic turret three stories high. She wasn't sure if it was the surprise, the shock, or the intense memories of their time together in that house, but seeing Brad standing there for the first time in all these years took her breath away.

Brad and the woman walked to the front door. She bent to dial a number into a lockbox and the door opened.

"That's Jeannie Marshall," Alex said.

"The realtor," Olivia said. An old classmate of her father's, Jeannie had gone out of her way to be kind after Olivia's mother left, occasionally dropping off meals and always trying to convince her dad to move to a new house, one with a view of the lake where he loved to fish.

"Not just a realtor—the top regional seller," Meg said. "Specializes in old, charming homes. Maybe Brad is looking to buy it?"

Olivia knew Brad's house next door to her was temporary, that he could afford one twenty times the size of the tiny bungalow. He could buy any house on earth—so why this one?

As she watched, a woman in a tight black skirt and high heels ran up the walkway and kissed Brad on the cheek. Olivia could tell from the sway of her hips and the flip of her black silky hair just who it was.

"Who's that other woman?" Meg asked. "Not a realtor, that's for sure."

"It's that reporter from *Live at Five*," Alex said, eyes bugging out. "What's her name again?"

"Erika Peters." Olivia blinked hard. Sexy Erika. Fun-loving, no-strings-attached Erika. The perfect woman to keep him company while he got away from all the complications that lived next door to him now.

Just what he said he wanted to do. Be carefree.

He guided Erika forward into the house with an arm on her back, the fire-engine-red door closing behind them.

Olivia heard the mental slam in her brain. How could he do it? Almost make love to her but then move so quickly to another woman?

Irritation smoldered in her chest like a newly crushed cigarette. A careful voice warned her she was being unreasonable. That her anger was out of proportion because the emotional and physical exhaustion of the past few weeks made her feel like she was having PMS on steroids.

Olivia turned to her friends, who sat wearing concerned looks. "I need to ask a favor. Could . . . you watch Annabelle for a few minutes?"

Did she just ask that out loud? Oh, God, what was she thinking?

Alex and Meg glanced at each other in that worried way only best friends can, until Alex finally spoke. "Olivia, are you sure you know—"

She stood up. "I'm rational, yes. I know what I'm doing."

Not really, but she was going to do it anyway.

Meg rushed to her side and gently tugged her sleeve. "Honey, maybe you shouldn't—"

"Look, a few minutes ago you both were warning me not to pass up my chance with Brad."

"That was before you were mad as hell," Alex pointed out.

She wasn't. Only her limbs quaked and black spots danced in front of her vision, and she ground her jaw so tight it might crack. A primordial need possessed her to get to him and see for herself what the hell was going on over there. Just when she thought she'd discovered the Brad she used to know, he was confirming all the womanizing, foot-loose, fancy-free stereotypes about him.

Calm down, calm down, her inner voice urged. She sucked in a few ragged breaths.

Olivia's heart squeezed with the revelation that all her passion had absolutely nothing to do with that house and everything to do with Brad.

Before she could process, her feet were crossing Main Street and marching through the wrought iron gate that surrounded the yard.

CHAPTER 14

Olivia stopped in front of the door, arm suspended in midair over the tarnished brass knocker. She was being foolish and she should leave. But then a vision sprung into her mind of Brad walking out this very door in pajama bottoms, picking up the rolled paper from the lawn, pouring coffee in the kitchen and then making love to Erika in that turret bedroom.

Olivia clutched the knocker and rapped it hard.

No answer.

She squinted up at the imposing red brick structure, with its soothing trim colors of green and gray. The color scheme wasn't working for her today. Tiptoeing to the nearest window, ignoring overgrown grass and weeds, she used her hands to shield her eyes. Window after window offered a glimpse of big, beautiful rooms with long-planked wood floors and fancy moldings, all of which loomed dark and empty.

Finally she spied Brad walking through an archway into what looked like a large dining room. Olivia bent low, but it was impossible to peek in due to a vast window well shielded by a waist-high, intricately carved iron railing. The iron looked a bit rusty but heavy and strong. It rattled a little as she slipped her feet cautiously between the rails so she could lean over and catch a glimpse.

An ornate chandelier dangled from the high dining room ceiling. The realtor, Erika, and Brad were gathered in the middle of the room, talking. Brad pointed upward, probably saying something about the intricate plaster ceiling medallion.

Until he saw her. A frown spread over his handsome face as he stared at her through the dusty window.

Busted.

Olivia jerked backwards, her running shoe wedging firmly between the iron posts of the railing. She twisted it to pull free, but her foot wouldn't budge.

More tugging. And grunting. Desperate, she twisted her foot until at last it pulled free from her shoe. But now the other shoe was stuck. Suddenly, the railing collapsed. The rusty bolts that anchored the railing into the concrete popped and it gave way, collapsing toward the window well. Her cell phone dropped, landing four or five feet down on a bed of rotting leaves.

Olivia pitched forward, ass over teakettle, and all she could do was cling to the railing with all her strength.

Strong arms grabbed hold of her just as she toppled over, pulling her by her yoga pants.

She could feel Brad's cool hand on her butt as he clutched a handful of the stretchy fabric. By now, he was bending over, too, and she was clutching the rails, struggling to right herself. But she couldn't. Below her, the ground was still a good four feet away from her head. If she dropped, she'd probably be okay, landing in a bed of decaying leaves sprinkled with a hefty helping of bugs, spiders, and rodents. She shuddered, from that thought or Brad's grip, she wasn't sure.

"Maybe we should call the Mirror Lake Rescue Squad," he said.

That would be the last thing she needed, to have this incident spread through town more rapidly than the plague, and last twice as long. She twisted around to catch a glimpse of Brad's face. He was biting back a smile. "God, Brad, just pull me up!"

"I'd rather stay here with my hand on your ass. Nice thong, by the way. Red, huh?"

Oh my God. "Don't call the police. Please. I'll never hear the end of it."

"Honey, it's not my fault you've taken to stalking me and got yourself in trouble." He paused. "I should let them come just to teach you a lesson."

His tone told her he was kidding. As she clung onto the slanted railing, she remembered what started all this in the first place.

"Is it true?" Olivia blurted. "You're buying the house?"

"Right now we're just looking."

We. That one tiny syllable crumbled Olivia's hopes faster than week-old coffee cake. Hopes she didn't even know she possessed. Every stupid retort she and Brad had shared seemed like a luxury now, something said in place of the truth.

Bitterness welled over. "Well, this is a great home for a family. Lots of room for kids to play in that big old yard and leave their bikes and balls scattered all around. That parlor was just made for a big old Christmas tree. And I hear the master bedroom's positively orgasmic."

"I should let go right now," he growled. "What's gotten into you? Are you angry with me for the other day?"

She squirmed a little under his hand. "No. Well, maybe. Mostly I'm angry at you for *right now.*"

"For looking at this old house?"

"It deserves a loving family."

She imagined him frowning. "What makes you think we're not a loving couple?"

Olivia's heart plummeted to her throat. "It's just like you to move in with somebody who wants you for one thing."

"And what might that be?" He sounded amused.

She twisted her neck just to shoot him a look of pure exasperation. "You know what—*sex.*"

"At least I know how to have fun. You probably pick your boy-friends based on their reading lists."

She tried to wiggle out of his grasp but he had her good and hard. "At least I pick men who are intelligent, not just good in bed."

Brad's shadow loomed over her, strong and menacing. "Why do you care if I'm with Erika?" Behind him, hundreds of mustard-colored dandelion heads bobbed like the poppies in Oz. "And don't tell me it's because we don't have a carload of kids to terrorize the neighborhood."

"What you do is your business." Olivia lifted her chin to a stub-born tilt and sniffed, which was hard to pull off in her current position. "I really don't care."

Oh, but she did. She'd lost him once and barely survived. And this time, she'd done it again, and it had nothing to do with her job and her leaving. She'd wasted so much time wrapped up worrying about how things could never work out between them, that Brad had taken mat-ters into his own hands. He'd chosen Erika over her.

Brad tapped a palm to his head in a light-bulb-going-off gesture. "You came hightailing it over here because you didn't want me to buy this house and move in with another woman. Because you and I made love here. Because you're *jealous*."

She winced at the word. "I am *not* jealous—no! Of course not." She turned her head away so he couldn't see her flaming face or her broken heart. "But just saying, it might be bad karma," she tossed over her shoulder.

He dropped his voice. His outstretched hand still clamped tightly on her butt. The damp, musty smell of dead leaves loomed close. "I just want to make sure I've got this straight. You're telling me it's bad luck to move in with another woman to the house we made love in ten years ago. Is that right?"

"It's . . . disrespectful." Her cheeks felt like radiant heaters. Oh, God, what had she just done? She might as well bolt for New York right after this, because she'd never face him again.

That was when she heard a laugh. The deep, from the belly, throw-your-head-back-and-laugh kind.

She wanted to kill him. It was a full-out, rumbling laugh that started deep down inside and overtook his whole body. She hadn't heard him laugh that way since back in high school when the zipper on her prom dress broke and he had to help her safety pin it together. That is, after he'd tucked his hands under the folds of her dress and took his time exploring what was inside.

"Go ahead, whoop it up," she said, bile in her voice. "I mean, who does that? *No one.* It's got to be bad luck."

"Just to set the record straight," Brad said, his lips tugging up in the slightest smile, "Erika wanted me to see the house for the possibility of converting it into a bed and breakfast. A business opportunity."

"What?"

"You heard me."

A business proposition, not a sexual one. She'd acted like a fool. Worse, she'd been outraged enough to stomp over in a fit of jealousy over a woman.

A woman who wasn't *her.*

The front door closed and the *click-clicking* of high heels sounded on the walkway.

"Oh my God, Brad, who is that?" Erika asked. Her voice sounded more shrill than sexy.

"Olivia. Her name is Olivia," he said darkly as he yanked hard on her pants, pulling her closer until he could grasp her waist in his big hands and tug her quickly up and onto safe ground.

He held her steady and secure as she fought off the dizziness from being upside down for so long.

Jeannie rounded the corner. "Olivia Marks? What in the world . . ."

"Hi, Jeannie." Olivia gave the realtor a little wave.

"This woman fell into the window well," Erika said, then turned her gaze on Olivia. "Were you like, spying on us?"

"Of course not," Olivia said. "I'm an editor. I'm researching Victorian ironwork and I was taking a photo." Okay, so it was the only thing she could come up with. That was plausible, right?

Brad shot her an incredulous look. Maybe not so plausible, but she was desperate.

"So you stood on it and it fell in?" Erika was aghast, her tone measuring high on the snark-o-meter.

"Just so long as you're all right, dear," Jeannie said, patting her arm.

"I'm fine," Olivia managed. "I'll see if my dad can come fix this."

"I've only got a few minutes before I have to get back to work," Erika said to Brad. "Mind if I finish walking through myself?"

Brad nodded. "I'll call you tomorrow."

"Just make sure the door locks behind you when you leave," Jeannie said.

Erika gave Jeannie a nod, pecked Brad on the cheek, and left, her hips swaying provocatively in her tight black skirt.

"Speaking of your father," Jeannie said, "I've been trying to get him to take a look at this cute little place on the other side of the lake." The words barely registered in the midst of all Olivia's shame and humiliation. Next to her, Brad was scowling and practically quivering with anger. Or laughter. Probably both. And he still hadn't let go of her waist, which disconcerted her even more. "Maybe you can convince him to come take a peek," Jeannie continued. "It's got a fishing pier and a screened porch to die for."

"I'll be sure to mention it," Olivia said.

Jeannie checked her watch. "I'm showing my daughter and her husband a property on the other side of the lake. Brad, would you mind giving me a ride over there? My car won't be out of the shop till tomorrow."

"No problem. It's right on my way home." Brad smiled and nodded a curt good-bye. As he slid his hands off her waist, he left behind a cold void.

Olivia nodded mindlessly as she watched Brad and Jeannie walk down the brick walkway to the street. Her mind was in a tailspin that had nothing to do with the rush of blood to her head.

Running over here had nothing to do with preventing sacrilege to an old house. She could tell herself that every day till she was old, hunched over, and wrinkled, but it was a lie. The real truth surged toward her like floodwaters through a broken dam.

She was completely and helplessly in love with Brad Rushford.

CHAPTER 15

"Naïve, innocent kids," Olivia mumbled a short while later as she sat on a park bench across from the square, watching a photographer shoot pictures of smiling prom couples under the flower-laden arbor. "If they knew what was good for them, they'd run." Alex and Meg sat beside her. Annabelle, thank goodness, slept soundly on Meg's shoulder. Brenda, the owner of Curli-Q, the salon behind them on the square, had wandered out of her shop to see what was going on.

"Here, honey, drink this down." Alex handed Olivia a plastic cup. "How's your ankle?"

Olivia held up a hand to say no to the drink. "It's just a little twisted. I'm fine—just suffering from a bad case of stupidity." Alex nudged the drink at her until Olivia finally grasped it. As soon as she took a sip, she gagged and clenched her throat to quell the liquid fire. "Good God, what is this?"

"It's my secret stash. Thought you might need some." Brenda patted Olivia on the arm, displaying her perfectly lacquered shiny red nails. "If it helps, I think you did the right thing, confronting your ex in front of that other woman."

"Thanks, Brenda, but it wasn't nearly that dramatic." But it would be tomorrow, after it had ground through the gossip mill and turned into how she'd declared her eternal love to Brad and threatened to drive Erika from town.

Olivia squeezed her hand in thanks. Brenda had styled Meg's and Alex's and her hair for years, and all their mothers' hair before that. She had a front-row seat for all the best drama of Mirror Lake.

Brenda went back in her shop for a refill just as a tall man wearing a beard and a large scowl walked up. Benjamin Rushford wore green scrubs and tennis shoes, likely fresh off a shift from his residency program in Hartford.

No one said anything. "Why do I get the feeling there is some serious female issue going on here?" Ben asked, cracking the infamous Rushford smile. He lifted the empty cup from Olivia's hand and smelled it. "And there's liquor involved."

Olivia shrugged, lacking the inclination to explain. Next to her, Meg stiffened. She'd probably fall silent, her usual response to Ben's presence.

Instead, Meg stood up carefully, cradling Annabelle so as not to disturb the sleeping baby. Giving no more than a quick nod of acknowledgment in Ben's direction, she spoke to Olivia, a frown casting shadows on her pretty features. "As your friend, I'm entitled to say that sometimes you need a kick in the butt, and right now, you could really use one."

Ben raised a brow, undoubtedly wishing he'd left when he had the chance.

Alex heaved a sigh. "She's right, Olivia. Brad just told you he's not buying that house with Erika. So what's holding you back?"

Ben's cell phone rang to the tune of Journey's "Any Way You Want It." "I just want to say I've never been more grateful to get a phone call." He answered the phone. "She's right here. No, I have no idea what happened. All right, Gran. Well, I have a date and I'm twenty-seven years old, but no, I won't stay out too late."

He repocketed the phone. "Effie wants to know what happened between you and Brad."

Alex patted Olivia's shoulder. "Word travels fast in Mirror Lake."

"I'm going to get the stroller out of your car and wheel Annabelle home to have a visit with my mom," Meg said. "She's been begging to see her. Would that be all right? You can pick her up later."

Ben held out his arms. "Let me take her and walk you to the car. I'll do anything to help break this tense mood."

"Actually, she *is* a bit heavy." Meg handed Annabelle over.

Ben adjusted the baby awkwardly. "I'm not so sure how to hold her."

Meg cast him a wary look. "Don't you deliver babies as part of your medical training?"

"Yeah, but I pass 'em off just as soon as I get them. Like a football." He made an awkward football-catching gesture with his hands with the baby tucked into the crook of his arm. Then he turned to Annabelle and chirped, "You're not much bigger than a football, are you, sweetheart?"

Meg helped adjust Annabelle, lifting her head a little and positioning Ben's arms more comfortably around the baby. "Actually, she's more the size of a muffler."

The comparison wasn't an accident. Ben was constantly working on his refurbished 1967 Mustang convertible.

"I see. Pretend she's an auto part. Great suggestion, Meggie." He grinned widely. "I can help you get the stroller and walk you to your house if you want. I'm going right by that way."

Meg hesitated. "Don't you have a date?"

"Just meeting some of my guy friends, but not till ten."

"All right, then, that would be nice." She turned to her friends on the bench. "Guess we'll see you all later."

Olivia mouthed a grateful *thank you* as Meg departed with Ben. Having some time to herself to think would soothe her prickled nerves.

Alex harrumphed. "That's the first time I've ever seen Meg actually talk with him."

"She's not that shy."

"Only around him."

They watched silently as the tall man and the petite woman walked away past the square.

"So what did Brad say?" Alex demanded.

Olivia scanned her friend's face. She was past the point of hiding the truth. "He's not buying the house with Erika. He was looking at it for business reasons."

Alex rubbed her arm. "Olivia, do you realize what you've done?"

"Besides make a fool out of myself, act jealous and crazily posses-sive of a house I don't even own, and show half the town I'm insane?"

"Besides all that."

"I really can't think of anything else more humiliating at the moment."

"You've just shown Brad you care for him—sort of." Alex lowered her voice till it sounded unusually gentle. "Now go talk to him."

"I've thought about this a lot, Alex. Both of us are terrified of change. Brad's spent a long time taking care of other people and I have no idea what my life would be like without my job."

"Think hard, Olivia. You've always been creative. New York isn't that far away." She paused thoughtfully. "Besides, look at it this way. Your life has changed whether you want it to or not. What's a little more?"

Olivia stared at her dream house. In the big side yard, fireflies blinked their neon-green signals. Olivia imagined a gaggle of kids in that yard, playing hide-and-seek, picking blackberries, and roasting marshmallows around a fire pit.

It was a beautiful fantasy, but one that could never be unless they could find some middle ground.

"Look at me," Alex said, her tone changed back to no-nonsense and insistent, giving Olivia no choice but to obey. She grabbed Olivia by both arms like a packet of Shake 'n Bake and shook her.

"I'm telling you this as one of your oldest friends. Sometimes a dream needs altering. Love means compromise. Your mother didn't compromise. She didn't know how."

Olivia stared at her friend. She was right. Her mother's misery had in large part been due to a tendency to see things as black or white, yes or no, either/or.

"Everyone has to make their own choices, Olivia. Don't be so afraid to examine the possibilities."

Olivia stood and hugged Alex. She wished things were as simple as Alex made them sound. "Thank you for being a good friend."

"You want a lift to Meg's? We can cruise by my house and grab dinner. Tom made a giant pot of mac and cheese for the kids."

"I need a good walk. But thanks again. I'll call you."

Olivia sat for a minute, watching Alex walk back to the diner. Couples strolled around the square, the big frosted globes on the lampposts turning on in the dusky light. On the wide sidewalk, someone walked two little dogs. The sharp aroma of good, strong coffee drifted up as an elderly couple passed, holding their cups from Mona's on the way to a bench. Olivia got up and cut across the square toward Meg's mom's house but stopped short in front of the old Victorian one last time.

What was it about old houses? They held endless mysteries between their walls yet were familiar and comforting, maybe because they lasted over all the hardships of time. Their craftsmanship couldn't be duplicated. Their uniqueness made all the effort of upkeep worth the trouble.

Kind of like Brad.

Olivia's father would disagree. He knew all about the leaking basements, the rotted beams, the constant maintenance. That's probably why Olivia had grown up in a nondescript 1970s ranch. After her mother left, her father didn't have time for an old house that took as much care as his children.

One of the prom kids had stuck a wrist corsage in the center of the wrought iron gate. White roses—the symbol of youthful innocence. Their sweet fragrance mixed with the sharp, exotic scent of the boxwood hedge that encircled the property.

On impulse, Olivia walked through the gate into the deserted side yard. An abandoned screened porch was empty, one of the screens slashed, and she stepped easily through. The porch connected to a long room with a fine wood floor and a big fireplace. But Olivia saw more than a dusty bare room.

She smelled Christmas pines and baking cookies, heard dogs barking and toddlers pushing toys and lugging baby dolls across carpets onto big comfy couches. She heard good-night stories being whispered to children almost asleep in their beds. She saw a bare-chested man in jeans drinking coffee and reading the Sunday paper, and in her daydream he looked like Brad.

It was foolish to enter the house, especially at dusk when the light would soon be scarce. Olivia's hands trembled as she clutched the chipped paint of the lower window sash.

For a moment, Olivia lowered her head on her arm. She was so tired. It wasn't from the jumble of events that had tossed her life around like clothes in a dryer, made it become a spinning merry-go-round out of control.

It was her life in general that had run amuck. She hadn't realized how much she'd needed her friends. And they'd been right by her side since the moment she'd arrived. Just now, Meg had taken Annabelle without hesitation. They both had kicked her butt when she needed it.

She was lonely. She loved her job, but she wanted more. Something to fill the hollowness inside. Something this house gave her.

She tugged on the sash. Paint splintered and peeled under her fingers, protesting her intrusion. To her surprise, the window opened and she was inside in a flash. Another minute later, she'd scaled the wide staircase and stood in the master bedroom doorway.

The room where she and Brad had first made love so long ago.

CHAPTER 16

Brad was a little out of breath by the time he'd climbed through the open window off the screened porch and took the stairs with unilateral purpose.

Part of him wanted to find Olivia and wring her neck.

But the rest of him wanted to stop wasting precious time. He wanted to claim her, kiss her senseless, and generally have his way with her until they were both too tired to mount an argument over anything except for who was going to make the morning-after omelet.

And this time, he wasn't taking no for an answer.

In seconds he stood in the doorway of the big master bedroom. Musty, shut-up house smell abounded, making him want to throw up the sashes of all the double-hung windows. He took in the big fireplace, the rounded contours of the turret that someone more feminine would say would make a great sitting area.

All thoughts fled as he saw Olivia sitting on the window seat, chin on her knees, looking out over their old hometown. Her fingers mindlessly stroked the ancient crushed velvet beneath her.

"It's that same purple color," he said.

She startled. Brad leaned against the door with his arms crossed, trying to look unaffected, but at that moment, in the dim light from the gathering night, she'd never looked so heart-stoppingly gorgeous. And it wasn't just the old memories playing tricks on his mind, of her at eighteen in the flush of youth. It was the Olivia of the here-and-now, the one with all the openhearted love for his baby niece, all her determination and resolve, and her smart-assed-comeback self, that he wanted so desperately.

"You mean mauve," she said. "Plum. Violet. Victorians probably wouldn't say purple." She was rambling, a sure sign she was nervous. Discombobulated. Good, because he wanted her off balance, without her defenses, without the sarcastic barbs she traded so well. He wanted to wear her down for the truth.

"How did you know—" she asked.

"You were here? I saw you walk into the porch and thought I'd make sure you didn't get stuck somewhere with your ass hanging out needing some help." Before she could zing him back, he cut her off. "But don't worry, from what I saw today, it's still a great ass."

Brad grinned and sat down opposite her, running his hand over the soft, heavy material. He placed his hand carefully over her much smaller one. He gathered it up, its size and softness striking him in an elemental way. At the sudden contact, she looked up. Beneath her pensive expression, a tsunami of questions stirred.

He ignored them. "I remember this velvet around your hair. You were lying there, your hair spread out, curls everywhere." He had to stop, because the words caught in his throat.

He reached over and touched her cheek, traced a line down her jaw with one finger. She shuddered. He wanted to ease her down slowly onto the soft cushion and start making some brand new memories. But first he had to clear the air. "Why did you really come storming over to talk to me today?"

Olivia left the window seat and walked across the room to the fireplace. Her hand skimmed over the darkly varnished mantel. "You know how I feel about . . . about this house. It's always been special to me."

Brad's footsteps echoed on the wood floor. He stopped close behind her, so near he could smell her lemony fragrance.

Nervously, she flattened her hand and pushed it across the polished wooden surface. As she slid her fingers across the fine old wood, they caught under the edge.

She gasped. Her shoulders stiffened. She swallowed hard and turned around.

Brad crossed the last step between them and wrapped an arm around her waist. But he didn't hold or kiss her as she might have anticipated. He reached out his other hand to the mantel. His fingers covered hers, traced over hers, felt the rough jagged-tooth ridges of the old carving just under the right edge.

"I forgot about this."

"So did I," she whispered. "For a long time."

He smiled. "After all these years, it's still there." He couldn't see it, but he remembered the words he'd carved himself. BRAD LOVES LIV 4 EVER.

Her eyes teared. "I couldn't stand the thought of you sharing this house with someone else. I thought I'd lost my chance with you forever. Erika's fun and uncomplicated and spontaneous and I'm none of those things."

He cradled her cheek, looked deeply into her soft, brown eyes, finally filled with pure honesty. "She's nothing to me. Nothing. I want you."

⊱─━━◦◦━━─⊰

Olivia stood frozen in the dusky room, her eyes riveted on the man who stood before her, the concentrated intensity of his powerful stare blazing between them. *I want you. She's nothing to me.* The simple truth flooded her heart and burst through the last remaining wall that held them apart. Her entire body quivered, her blood running hot and cold with need. She wanted him, had always wanted him, and nothing, nothing would stop them from being together now.

Brad leaned toward her, effectively enclosing her between taut, lithe muscle and the hard edge of the wood. The brick of the fireplace scraped roughly against her palms as she clutched desperately for balance. He was too large, looming, all broad shoulders and big arms, his cologne enveloping her with its seductive richness.

He branded her with his lips, sliding them over hers and invading her mouth with his tongue. Stroke after silky stroke reduced her to a molten, boneless heap. Her legs buckled, flimsy as rubber bands. She grasped at him to steady herself, fisting the crisp cotton of his shirt.

He pushed her up against the wall, the hard length of him straining against her inner thigh. Her hips thrust against him and her tongue tangled with his, eager to meet all his demands with her own.

"God, I missed you," she choked out on a sob.

Brad lifted his head, grasped her shoulders, and locked his gaze onto hers.

Olivia stared, unable to think. Her arms tingled where his hands stroked her hot skin. She had never been so aroused. Why, oh why, had he stopped?

He smiled against her mouth, hovered over it, teasing her lower lip between his teeth. "You're worrying me. No quips? No zingers?"

"No one has driven me more crazy, in a good and a bad way," she managed.

"That's better. Now you're back to being feisty."

In one swift movement, he pulled off his shirt and tossed it behind him, exposing hills and valleys of golden perfection.

"We fight a lot," she said weakly as he undid one button after another on her blouse. His fingers scalded her tender flesh. She arched her back, giving him full access.

"I prefer the term *negotiate*."

"See?" she said breathlessly. "We don't even agree on what word to use."

"Then we'll have to find other things to agree on." Her blouse dropped away. He pushed a bra strap down and took one pink nipple between his teeth. Sensation zinged through her straight to her groin and she pushed against him to try and ease the desperate void only he could fill. She ran her hands along his broad back, reveling in the feel of his warm skin stretched over tight muscle.

"I don't want you after all," she said. "You're too complicated."

Mischief twinkled in his eyes. "You love complicated. Otherwise you'd be bored."

"Brad," she said, barely able to form the word. Her fingers tangled in his hair, so silky, both coarse and smooth, and curved against the back of his head. She leaned in, giving herself over to everything he offered.

"What is it?"

"I'm definitely not bored."

In response, he scooped her up and deposited her on the window seat. "Wait here," he said hoarsely. He ran to the doorway and reached into the hall, returning with a thick quilted blanket. "From my car."

"You knew?"

"I *hoped*." He captured her hand and led her over to the window seat, tossed the blanket over it and spun her about. "Take off your clothes."

"That sounds a little bossy," she said, kicking off her shoes and sliding down her yoga pants.

"Now, honey, you know I'd never ask you to do anything I wouldn't do myself."

All at once, he stood before her naked, all chiseled planes and carved muscle. The boy she knew, grown into this—the most gorgeous man she'd ever seen. A thrill shook her, and she uttered a prayer of thanks that somehow in the wide universe they'd found each other again after so long.

"You look . . . different."

"How so?" He swept his hand in front of his body, knowing damn well he possessed the build of Adonis.

Olivia skimmed her hands over his broad chest, enjoying the concrete hardness of his muscles, the soft feel of his tanned skin, and the light grazing of dark hair over his pecs. She shrugged. "Buff. Toned." She looked down. "Large."

He grinned.

"Oh, and humble. I forgot humble."

"You humble me, Olivia. Nothing in my life has ever felt so good or so right."

She reached for him. But he grazed her forehead with a quick kiss and reached under the blanket to pull out a condom, which he ripped open with his teeth and made quick use of. Then he pushed her back onto the seat and draped his delicious weight over hers.

A balmy breeze blew in from the window across her heated skin. In the square, Olivia was vaguely aware of the neon sign of Pie in the Sky, the evening crowds laughing and talking. In the distance, the church steeple lit up among mounds of trees. Landscape she'd looked at for most of her life but it suddenly seemed new and different.

He poised above her, looking deeply into her eyes. When she was eighteen, that look was a huge deal, and even after all these years, his eyes still held an intensity that rocked her down to her soul.

Brad smiled, waiting for her nod, "Olivia," he whispered, claiming her lips and her body. "I only ever wanted you."

His words struck her straight in her heart. She surrendered to him completely. Kisses came more urgently, thrusts heaved, intimate muscles clenched, and she lost sense of everything but the sensation of the two of them becoming one.

Her body remembered him and welcomed him as if no time had passed. They cried out on the same breath as they drank in each other's bodies, filled each other's minds and hearts in a release that was swift, shocking, and completely fulfilling.

Brad held her as the room fell dark, except for the soft glow of the lights in the park below. A gentle breeze stirred, cooling their heated bodies. He wished he'd brought a second blanket to shield Olivia from the night chill. He used his own warmth instead, drawing her close as they lay together, limbs entwined on the window seat.

"What are you thinking about?" she asked, her head on his chest, her fingers gently tracing the skin along his pecs.

"Our first time." He stared at the ceiling, but sought her hand, bringing it to his mouth and kissing her knuckles. "Want me to tell you about it?"

She shifted to look at him. Her hair was tumbled all over his chest, long waves of glorious, silky softness that he wanted to inhale and tangle his fingers in forever. "Depends what you're going to say."

"It was raining. We ran in here and the sky let loose." He fingered a strand of her hair. "When I saw you all wet from the shower the other day, that's what I thought of. How you looked that night."

Her hand gently stroked his cheek and he closed his eyes to revel in the warmth of it. "I never wanted anyone more than I wanted you at that moment," she whispered.

"When I first saw you naked, I couldn't stop shaking." He looked down at her. Took in her beautiful brown eyes. Placed her hand over his heart. "Olivia, I'm shaking now."

Tears shone in her eyes. He had a lot more he wanted to say, but he didn't want to break the magic. He didn't want anything to ruin this night. So he wrapped his arms around her and rested his chin atop her head. Kissed her beautiful hair. And thought what a lucky son of a bitch he was to have gotten a second chance at the most perfect love of his life.

CHAPTER 17

Bacon. The smoky-strong aroma reached Olivia from the foldout bed in the spare room where she slept. She yawned and stretched, enjoying the warmth of sunlight sneaking in below the shade and spilling onto the sheets. In the daze of half sleep, she felt perfectly cozy and content. And naked.

Naked?

Consciousness ratcheted her awake. Her eyes flew open. The sun was intense, way too bright for early morning.

Annabelle. Her blood froze. Fear made her bolt upright. The baby always awakened at least once before her usual rising time at dawn. Olivia remembered doing certain things during the night but feeding Annabelle was definitely not one of them. Kicking back the covers and grabbing her robe, she sped down the hall to the kitchen.

Brad sat at the table holding Annabelle. Relief made her teary, but shock made her wonder if she were still dreaming. Even from behind, she could see two plates heaped full of bacon and fluffy scrambled eggs. Unaware she was there, Brad bit off a piece of toast and chattered to the baby, who looked at him with an enchanted look. "One day you'll eat bacon, too, little girl. Bacon makes you big and strong. And beautiful.

And you are going to be a knockout one day. But we won't even think about that for now. No boys for you till you're thirty."

"Brad." Olivia exhaled the word on a sigh of relief. She collapsed in the seat next to him, a hand over her pounding heart. "I was so frightened. I haven't slept an entire night since . . ."

"You needed it." His bright green gaze assessed her, intense as a sparkling Caribbean sea.

She tugged on her ratty robe and raked her hands through her rat-nest hair. Her morning-after image was probably enough to shatter glass.

Brad reached out a hand to stop her. "Don't. I like it like that."

She laughed and shook her head. "I'll scare the baby."

He brought his own hand up to finger a wayward curl. "You look . . . rested. Satisfied. Sexy as hell."

Oh my gosh, he just told her she didn't resemble Godzilla. He thought she was *sexy*.

Olivia didn't realize she was tapping her fingers on the table until he stilled her hand with his. Their gazes clicked and held, making her heart squeeze with an emotion she was afraid to identify—it was too good, too warm and wonderful.

She kissed Annabelle on the head and told her how adorable she looked in her yellow sleeper with footies. The baby flashed her a gummy smile and nestled her head against Brad's bare chest.

And a fine chest it was. Skin soft as Annabelle's over sinewy, tight muscle, lightly sprinkled with bronze hair that tracked in a line and disappeared into the waistband of his jeans. If he wasn't holding Annabelle, she would have jumped into his lap and devoured him for breakfast instead of the food. He was completely at ease, sipping coffee and feeding the baby, his bare feet crossed at his ankles, as if he did this every day of the week. Altogether, the sexiest man she'd ever laid eyes on.

She dared to imagine future scenarios like this one, lazy weekend mornings with a man who cared enough to let her sleep, who got up himself to care for the baby, who cooked her breakfast.

That was too unreal to believe, so she forced her thoughts on business. "Want me to take her?" It was the least she could offer after all he'd done.

"What I really want is for you to have breakfast. I made way too much food."

She took a bite of bacon. "I'm starving." She hadn't eaten bacon in years—never touched the stuff. But it was so delicious she savored every bite and reached for another.

"I'm starving, too," he said with a grin. "And I don't mean for food." He cupped her cheek in his warm, big hand and she felt like she would melt like the butter on her toast.

"It'll be *baby interruptus* unless we wait till naptime," she said.

"I can wait." She loved those little crinkles around his eyes. She wanted to trace every single one. And bask in this incredible feeling she hadn't felt since . . . well, since she was eighteen years old.

"Last night was . . . amazing. Spectacular," Brad said. He had this way of making her feel like she was, well, exactly that. And beautiful. Every one of her billion nerve endings hummed with happiness.

"I feel the same way."

"Olivia, I—"

A sharp rap sounded at the backdoor. Shielding his eyes against the glass of the door and peering inside was the face of her father.

Staring at her and Brad in all their post-lovemaking unruliness.

Oh. My. God.

She wanted to close her eyes and wish herself back to her New York apartment where no one poked into her business except occasionally Mrs. Bertolini and her Cocker Spaniel.

Her father saw her and waved. Olivia's first impulse was to scream *Run! Hide!* Like when they were caught necking afterhours in the school parking lot by the police chief. But she wasn't a teenager and Brad was anchored to the table by Annabelle. So Olivia sucked in a breath, pulled her robe together, and made her way to the door.

"Hi, Dad." Her voice sounded faint and riddled with guilt. She wedged her body between the doorframe and the door to block her dad's view of Brad, but she could tell by the shocked expression on his face that it was too late.

Her father looked past her shoulder. "Bradley."

Olivia heard Brad say "hi" as she fully opened the door and stepped back.

"Olivia," her father said with a nod. To his credit, he recovered his usual calm expression pretty quickly. "I brought you a replacement screen for that window. And I brought coffee, but it looks like you've already got some going."

Pecking him on the cheek, she took the cups from his hands. "You know I love Mona's. Come sit down."

She worried her lower lip. What must her father think of her, sleeping with Brad knowing she had to go back to New York in a couple days. *Bad judgment. A terrible error.*

Olivia tried to get up the steam to scold herself but just couldn't muster it. She felt too giddy, too happy. For once, she didn't try to apologize or ramble on. It was what it was, and whatever *that* was, it was between her and Brad.

Brad stood up with Annabelle out of respect. "Morning, Mr. Marks. As you can see, I made enough food to feed half of Mirror Lake. Hope you'll join us."

Frank Marks looked around. His gaze did a panorama of Brad's naked chest, Olivia's wild hair, Annabelle's drooly smile, and the spread of food at the table. He chucked the baby under one of her chins and sat down. "Well, I don't know about you all, but I'm starved."

Olivia blew out a pent-up breath. Brad poured an extra orange juice and set it on the table. When he said, "Let's eat while it's still warm," she flashed him a smile of gratefulness for being so welcoming to her crotchety dad. How could he sit there so unembarrassed, so at ease, when she was the exact opposite of calm and collected?

Unbelievably, her father filled his plate, wiggled his fingers for Annabelle, and vocalized some awkwardly silly sounds for her benefit. Olivia passed him a fresh cup of coffee.

He took a bite of eggs and pointed his fork at Brad. "You made these?"

"I took a bunch of cooking classes so I could select menus with my chefs. But truth is, I came to enjoy cooking."

Good-looking, great in bed, loves kids, cooks. The icing on the delicious, extraordinary Brad cake.

"Tasty eggs. But what are your intentions with my daughter?"

Olivia sputtered her coffee. The bacon she'd just scarfed churned sickly in her stomach. She had the sense that what she was about to hear would be life altering, and every cell halted its biological functions to listen.

Brad smiled, as unaffected as if her dad had just asked for his phone number. But on close inspection, a tiny muscle in his jaw throbbed. And the smile looked a little forced. He also took a bit longer than usual to reply. "Mr. Marks, I . . . have the greatest respect for you and your daughter. But I have to ask that you give us some time to figure that out."

Oh. Her heart stuttered, faltered a little. The bright, shining happiness that had filled her dimmed a little. But she put on a bright smile. "Let's eat, okay?"

Her dad shot her a glance that she knew to be fatherly concern, but he was kind enough to mumble something like "fair enough" and keep eating.

God, Brad had *hesitated.* He *never* hesitated.

She'd expected the Cinderella answer. Something like, "Mr. Marks, I'm in love with your daughter. Always have been, always will be."

Clearly, she was into the fairy tale and he wasn't. He'd warned her, of course, that day in Bridal Aisle. He'd accused her of always wanting the Disney ending.

An ending, apparently, he might not be capable of giving.

The few bites of eggs and toast she managed to choke down might as well have been chalk and dust. She made a few attempts at small talk, but mostly she just listened to Brad and her father talk about construction problems.

You're taking this too seriously.

That's right, she was. In that moment, Olivia realized that she'd unconsciously set up a vision of her life with Annabelle that had included family, friends, a home, a full life—and Brad.

Suddenly, her life in New York seemed way lacking.

But maybe he didn't share that. Maybe he'd just given in to the combustible attraction that always seemed to surround them like an aura. Perhaps she was no more than a bead on his string of women that he had fun with while he enjoyed his single, carefree life. Once again, she'd thought he'd cared—okay, *loved* her—and she couldn't be wrong. Or could she?

"Oh, I almost forgot," her father said over his second cup of coffee. He dug a Post-it out of his pocket and handed it to Olivia. "Joe and Beth Hastings have a daughter in New York who adopted a baby. They thought she might be able to give you some insights."

"Lots of people adopt babies, Dad." She wasn't sure how this particular person would help, except it was always good to meet potential friends for Annabelle.

"It was an unexpected adoption. Happened while they were waiting on another baby. They had one day to make a decision, without any time to prepare."

"What'd they decide?"

"They took the child—a girl. Then, nine months later, the other agency was finally ready. So they adopted a boy, too."

"Interesting. So they became parents suddenly, too." Without the benefit of months to prepare or adjust. Just like her.

She was about to ask him more when her cell rang. Olivia looked at the name on the screen and blinked. *Sylvia.*

Her boss was finally calling back.

Olivia's heart kicked up in nervous anticipation as she walked out of the kitchen and down the hallway for privacy. Sylvia knew she was tough and aggressive, had brokered increasingly larger deals, and had worked her way up to editorial director in six years. She was too good an employee to let go.

Hope bloomed in her chest. With a saner schedule, she could hire a great nanny and see Brad on weekends. Not the perfect solution, but doable. Maybe this could all work out.

"Olivia, I need you back ASAP." The cigarette-tainted grittiness of Sylvia's voice added an extra layer of harshness to her words. "Helen quit and Ryan Connor is threatening to leave the house. I'm sorry, but reducing your hours is out of the question now."

Olivia's heart, anchored by disappointment, sank to rock bottom. Icy fingers of fear pricked her spine. The rosy future that seemed within reach minutes ago was ripped away.

Her brain raced to process a hundred different emotions, all of which sucked. "Why did Helen quit?" she asked.

She knew why, even before Sylvia spoke. Her biggest author, Ryan Connor, was particular, quirky, and obsessive, and for most people, working with him was a trial. The only reason she could was because she understood him in an elemental way. He was a meticulous perfectionist and she got that. They'd actually become friends.

"Helen couldn't take the heat. Connor wants you back or he's pulling out. How soon can you get here?"

⊷••○••⊶

Brad found Olivia in the hallway, clutching the phone to her chest. He didn't have to guess the news was bad.

"Sylvia needs me back in New York right away." Her voice was a clotted whisper. "The author I've been working with for the past year is threatening to bail."

"The self-help guru?" Yeah, Brad knew who Ryan Connor was. Every colleague of his who wanted to be a success in business had a copy of his last book on their shelves, *The Assertiveness Project: Work Hard, Plan Hard, Get What You Want.* He'd made the rounds on every talk show, been written up in *People,* and his book was everywhere, from the big chain bookstores to Target.

She nodded. "Our biggest client. He's refusing to work with anyone else."

Brad paced the darkened hallway, his lighthearted mood dissolving in the dim light. He understood she had an important job. But what kind of employer did that to a new mother, especially under these circumstances? She needed more time to adjust, adapt, rest. He hated the thought of her jumping at her boss's call and even asking *how high.* Her eagerness to get back meant something he couldn't accept.

It was him versus the job, and he could already see which one won.

Brad clasped her by the arms, overpowered by a dark sense of desperation mixed with blind fury. "Fuck the client. Stay here and marry me. We'll give Annabelle a home and a family. You wouldn't have to worry about money or working unless you wanted to."

Olivia gasped. She looked shocked. Oh, hell, it had all come out so badly. A lukewarm proposal in the form of a demand and telling her she didn't need to work when he couldn't imagine her never working in her life. Brad's brain buzzed, stunned by his own outburst. On autopilot, he dropped to one knee, but even as he did it, his heart was breaking. It felt wrong. Like he was begging, not asking. He already knew her answer, and he couldn't bear to look.

Her fingers smoothed his hair and for a second he was comforted. Slowly, she slid her back down the wall until she sat next to him. Tears streaked her face like rivulets of rain down a windshield.

"I have to go back, Brad. I've invested my heart and soul in this project for over a year. Other people's jobs are at stake."

He shook his head fiercely, as if that would prevent the truth from penetrating. She wasn't even going to consider it working between them. Her life in New York was more important than he was.

Annabelle let out a cry. Olivia's father walked about the kitchen, trying to soothe her.

"I'll get her." Brad rose, relieved to have something else to do.

Somehow he went through the motions of thanking Frank for staying and mumbled some excuse about Olivia being tied up on the phone. Olivia changed Annabelle and put her down for a nap while he tackled the kitchen, the repetition of familiar tasks the only thing that prevented him from losing it.

Olivia came up behind him at the sink, encircled his waist with her arms. His gut clenched with desperation. "I love you," she said. "But please, please understand I have to do this."

Brad closed his eyes. Felt the warmth of her hands around his waist. Wished he could take back the past quarter hour and go back to the absolute joy he'd felt. Yet he knew from experience any "I love you" trailed by a "but" was not good. He turned, wiped his hands on the towel he'd slung over his shoulder.

Olivia looked pale and upset, but he held her at arm's length. "I don't know what to say. Except sometimes it seems like your job is more important than Annabelle or I are."

"No! It's not like that." Her beautiful brown eyes looked startled and sad. Even in his anger, he hated to see her hurt.

He squeezed his eyes shut, forcing the image out of his mind. "When we were kids, I got why you needed to leave. Back then we both let our differences overcome us. We're older now. We can fight for what we want."

"If you knew me at all, you would never ask me to give everything up so easily."

"Well then, maybe I don't really know you, Olivia." Because it sure seemed to him that she didn't have the slightest problem giving *him* up. That made her eyes tear up and she backed away. "While I'm there, I'll finalize the nanny. And once the book's done they'll drop my hours."

She sounded like she had a plan. Too bad he wasn't included. "What if they don't?" He swallowed hard. His words tasted as bitter as they sounded. "I'm sure this project will only be replaced by another one just as urgent."

"I know you're angry with me. But surely you don't expect me to up and quit everything I've worked ten years for?"

She reached out to him but he sidestepped her. If she touched him he'd be a goner. He tore a hand through his hair. "I'm trying to understand. I just don't get how you can sacrifice Annabelle in the process." *And me*, a voice inside his head whispered. But he would never say it.

"And sometimes I feel that Annabelle is your only concern."

"She's a helpless baby. She needs a family. Or have you forgotten she's already lost one of those?" He had to keep his focus on Annabelle. Because the pain of his own rejection threatened to break him in half.

Anger flashed in her eyes. "What do you want from me, Brad? Do you honestly think I'd quit my job, move back here and be just your wife?"

"Just my wife." His hands shook so he fisted them. He paced, sealed his lips and gnawed his cheek to prevent himself from saying things he'd regret as those three little words ping-ponged around his brain, each jolt a jarring stab. "Sometimes I think you forget that raising a child requires sacrifices. Ones you aren't willing to make."

A frown darkened her brow. "That's so unfair, Brad. Why does it have to be all-or-nothing? For you, it seems the only good solution is if I stop working and come back here to live."

"I never asked you to stop working. But what they're asking you to do is unreasonable. Why can't you push back a little, offer a compromise, something?" Her job loomed too large, like another person in their relationship.

He couldn't connect with her, couldn't see her way or make her see his. Her rejection of everything he'd just offered—of him—was complete.

"Go back to New York, Olivia," he ground out. "Finish your project. But who will watch Annabelle until you can hire a permanent person?"

"Most of my friends are single but I can make a few phone calls. I think I can make a temporary arrangement until I decide on the right nanny."

Brad's stomach clenched to think of Annabelle moved around again, taken care of by strangers. It just seemed . . . wrong.

"I know it's not ideal, but it's the best I can do on such short notice." Olivia walked to the back door and stared out at the lush green backyard. An uncomfortable silence settled between them.

"I'll take her," Brad blurted. "I'll take Annabelle." The words shocked him, even as they spilled from his mouth.

Olivia spun back toward him, her mouth open in surprise. "You'd take her? Temporarily, of course."

"I'd have to put her in daycare, but I've known Sally Hersch for years and I know she runs a quality place. My family can help me out here and there." He'd barely blinked an eye before replying, but it felt right. He adored Annabelle, he knew that much. Somehow, his need to be footloose, free of responsibilities, seemed distant and unimportant.

"How do you feel about that—I mean, independent of the problems we're having?" She stood in the middle of the kitchen, hugging her arms around herself, her mouth drawn into a thin, tense line.

He ached to make things right between them, but he had no idea how. "I would rather take care of her myself than see her switched from stranger to stranger."

"I-I would be comfortable leaving Annabelle with you, someone she knows and who loves her. It seems like the best solution—if you're okay with it."

"Why wouldn't I be okay with it? I meant what I offered." Even if he was so angry and upset with Olivia he couldn't see straight.

An ice-cold trickle of dread shot down his spine. In offering to take the baby, he was giving her time to reconsider Mirror Lake, motherhood, and him. Once she returned to New York, her familiar routine might knock all three right out of her thoughts for good.

"Well, I'm glad we have Annabelle taken care of." Her words carried a bite.

What did she want from him? He'd done his best to do the right thing, but he couldn't stomach a big declaration of love. Not when he was so damn angry and she was leaving him anyway. And maybe she wouldn't come back.

Brad rubbed a sudden crick in his neck as he set down the dishtowel and mumbled a quick good-bye. How had he done it? Allowed her back into his life, his heart. He was that eighteen-year-old kid again, staying behind while she left for the big city, his old heartbreak ripped wide open and bleeding again.

The door snapped shut behind him, separating him from the woman—the two women—he loved. Yes, it was the exact same pain as before.

Only doubled.

CHAPTER 18

"Why did you let her leave? How *could* you?" It was 8:00 a.m. and Samantha was in Brad's face, rattling him like she always did. Except he'd slept all of two hours and if he didn't get some coffee *right now*, he might just kill her.

And make it look like an accident.

It had been three days since Olivia left and agreed to leave Annabelle with him. She'd only been gone for two but Annabelle *knew*, and that made his heartburn flare worse than hot sauce on spicy wings. What must be going through her little baby mind? That nothing and no one was permanent? And apparently he wasn't the baby whisperer that he claimed to be, because she was not having any of his charms. She wanted Olivia.

He just prayed breakfast would calm her. If only he could find a clean bottle. Bouncing Annabelle in one arm while he prepared her formula with the other, he opened the microwave door but Samantha snatched the bottle from his hand.

"You're not supposed to do that. Here, let me help you." She took a pan out and began running some warm water.

Where was that damn coffee pot?

The counter was full of bottles, dishes. A pile of baby clothes lay in the middle of the kitchen floor, waiting to be put in the washer. His cell phone rang. Olivia had called—a lot—but finally he'd told her Annabelle was *fine, just fine*, and he needed some time and space to cool down. When he checked his phone, he found seven messages from the restaurant. Troubles abounded, no doubt because he'd been neglecting that, too. Fires smoldered everywhere.

He finally located the coffee pot among the fallout. One cold, grainy swig left. *Just his luck*. He drank straight from the pot.

For all his cocky arrogance, he certainly was not getting it together. How could he have ever criticized Olivia?

"So?" Samantha said accusingly, swirling the bottle in the warm water. "Why'd she leave?"

He shot his sister a murderous glare. Good thing she was too busy to notice. He didn't want to piss her off too badly or he'd have no help at all.

"It's complicated." Samantha was just a college kid. What did she know of adult problems anyway?

She spun around from the stove. "Quit treating me like a child. In case you haven't noticed, I'm not one anymore."

Like he needed one more person to fuel his massive headache. "Look, I know you're angry with me, but it was Olivia's decision to leave. She's got a job and a life and neither of those are here in Mirror Lake."

"Maybe they would be if you asked her to marry you."

He remembered his weak-kneed marriage proposal Olivia must have sensed as half-hearted. But then he remembered her insistence on leaving, and her rejection of him. "What are you talking about?"

"Or maybe you just want Annabelle all to yourself."

The final twig snapped, and with it his temper. "Now why the hell would I ever want that? Do you have any idea how hard it is to raise a kid *by yourself*? Especially when they buck you at every turn." *Like you.*

"Yeah, well, if you weren't so wrapped up with everything maybe you'd notice that something's wrong with me."

Brad looked at his sister—really looked. She *was* pale. Come to think of it, her eyes were kind of puffy and red. And she had dark circles under her eyes.

Oh, shit, something else he'd missed. He hadn't noticed. He'd been too wrapped up in his own problems.

He set the baby down in her playpen in the middle of the family room floor. She fussed a little but he cranked up some musical toy and that quieted her temporarily. Then he grabbed his sister by the arms.

"Sit down and I'll make you breakfast. We can talk. All right?"

A tear rolled down her cheek but she nodded and sat. "I'm not hungry."

"Are you sick?" *Please, God, don't be pregnant.* The bitter, acidic coffee he just drank roiled in his stomach. "Just sit." He snatched a box of Kleenex from the counter, got the bottle and the baby, and sat with Samantha at the table.

"Spike and I broke up."

He released a sigh of relief. *But please, please don't be pregnant.* "I'm sorry about that," he managed. He was sorry, for her pain, anyway. But not for the breakup.

"Well, you were right about him. When I wouldn't sleep with him, he dumped me." A tear formed in the corner of her eye and she swiped at it.

Brad's shoulders sank, half from relief that she hadn't slept with him, half because he'd failed his sister again. He'd been wrapped up in his own misery, didn't even see hers. This job was a never-ending spiral of screwups, each one worse than the last. He reached out a hand and rubbed her back as she cried with her head down on the table.

"Honey, look." What was he supposed to say? That some things are better over? That she'd find someone far better than that idiot? He chose higher ground. "There's no one I know who didn't get their heart broken some time or another."

"He said . . . he said I was boring. He said I was a virgin tease. Oh, Brad, I'm never going to find anyone who just loves me . . . for me."

She was hiccupping and crying and she was a hot mess. He usually avoided crying women at all costs. The boys never cried, except when the dog died, and he was grateful for their general lack of roller-coaster drama. But tears made him feel worse than helpless. He handed her another Kleenex and she blew her nose.

If Olivia were here, what would she say? He wracked his brain and came up with, "You're perfect just the way you are, and if he doesn't realize that, it's his loss." *The son of a bitch. And if he comes near you again, I'll kill him.*

"He said he was sick of hearing about my career dilemmas and life crises and told me it would be best if we broke up."

"When you really love somebody, you stick with them through thick and thin and you'll do anything not to let that person go."

Even as he said the words, he winced. *God, he was a dumb fuck.* Misery seeped through every pore. "If Spike really loved you, he'd want to hear about your life. Relationships are all about give and take. Maybe the reason Spike doesn't want to talk is because he's more interested in getting something else."

"Brad!"

"Look, I'm your oldest brother. And I can't help wanting to watch over you and protect you. Everything I've ever done, whether I've done it well or badly, has been because I love you and want you to have a great life. And if I see that someone might not want you for the right reasons, I'm going to say something about it, whether you want me to or not."

"I thought Spike loved me. How do you know—when someone really loves you?"

"They put your needs first. They know you so well, they understand what's really important to make you happy. And when you both disagree, you find a way to compromise."

If only relationships were that easy. Maybe he hadn't understood how important Olivia's job was to her. Maybe he hadn't put himself totally on the line for her. But maybe neither of them was good at compromise.

"Brad, maybe I was relying too much on Spike. There's something going on at school I haven't told you about."

He steeled himself for whatever was coming. Reminded himself that as long as she wasn't pregnant, he could handle just about anything else.

"I went back to school after the funeral but I—well, I couldn't concentrate and I tried to study for my exams but I was upset a lot so I didn't even take two of them and the other two I got really bad grades on. I know you're going to be so disappointed in me, but my professors said I can retake them and still keep my GPA up. I'm sorry, Brad."

He looked hard at his little sister. Misery filled her every pore. She was worried about pleasing him, failing him. He'd sent her back to school after Kevin's death thinking she'd get through it. She'd been so upset she couldn't concentrate and she hadn't even told him until now.

He gathered her to him and tucked her head under his chin like he used to when she was little. He wrapped his arms around her slender shoulders and squeezed tight. He felt tears dampen his shirt.

"I'm the one who should be sorry." When he'd worked three jobs and went to school, he'd barreled forward in a haze of sleep deprivation. But he hadn't lost his brother. When had he become perceived as a taskmaster who had to be pleased at any cost?

"I'm sorry I didn't see your grief. And I'm sorry you were suffering by yourself and didn't feel comfortable enough to call me. I've done a lot of things wrong with raising you. Mostly, I'm sorry you got me and not Mom and Dad."

She lifted her head, her face all red and blotchy and tear-streaked, her eyes round and big. It reminded him of when she was three years old, listening to him rapturously as he embellished stories about Santa and the Easter Bunny.

Except she was far beyond that, and he needed to start treating her like she was. He snorted. "I made every mistake in the book. I was too hard on you. I tried to crush your defiance and that was like throwing water on a kitchen fire. The more I tried to squelch it, the more defiant you got. I felt out of control, and it was the only way I knew."

She placed a cold, clammy hand over his and he grasped it like there was no tomorrow. "You're never out of control."

"Honey, you have no idea. I always pretended to know what I was doing in front of all of you. Underneath, I was scared shitless."

Her lips tipped up in a half smile. "This is the first adult conversation we've had."

"I love you, Sam. I'm sorry you got stuck being raised by me and not our real parents. They were . . . awesome. They knew what a real family was."

"So do you," she said very softly.

"You know, after Effie got sick, that lawyer threatened to split us up. They wanted to send you to Great-aunt Agnes's and the boys to Uncle Stan on the farm in Iowa."

She raised one elegant brow. "I could have gone with Great-aunt Agnes? The old cat lady in Vermont?"

"That was the plan. Until I got two other jobs and Effie got Doc Collins to say she was a whole lot healthier than she was."

"Oh, Brad." She got up and threw her arms around him. The scents of fruity shampoo and gum wafted up. Funny how she looked more and more like a woman but still smelled like a teenager. "I guess I always resented I had to listen to you—my brother—instead of having real parents. I know I gave you a hard time, and I'm sorry."

Something Olivia said echoed in his head. "You were just being a teenager. It's all right." He patted her hand, stroked her curls. Silently begged for the waterworks to stop. "And I've been thinking . . . you should go ahead and apply to art school. It's what you love, and it makes you happy."

She lifted her head, her eyes puffy but incredulous. "You said that's not a good enough reason to pick a career, that I have to think of business things, too. Being financially secure. Making money."

"Well, I was wrong. All the money in the world won't do a thing if you get up every day and hate yourself. Follow your dream." God, that was tough. But somehow he did it, cut the balloon tether so she could soar.

"I love you. I'm so glad you're my brother." Tears soaked the shoulders of his T-shirt.

"Me, too." He chuckled a little at his own joke. "But please stop crying now."

In that moment, he realized love could make up for a whole lot of mistakes. His youth and inexperience. His confusion in being a parent. At least he certainly hoped so, because he loved each of his siblings with all his heart.

But with Olivia he'd held back. Blown the marriage proposal. Pushed against a wall, he'd panicked and there was no reason to believe she'd take that unromantic horseshit he'd tossed at her seriously. Especially when it contained words like *you don't have to work* when it was clear she loved her job. No wonder she'd rejected him.

He'd been afraid. Of putting himself out there. Of being out of control. Of being *left*. Well, here he was anyway, no better off than before.

Way to go, rocket scientist.

"I asked Olivia to marry me but it was bad. I didn't even tell her I loved her."

"Maybe she thought you were asking her for Annabelle's sake, not for her, you know?"

He shrugged. Maybe he had hidden behind Annabelle to avoid expressing his real feelings. With each passing day, he feared Mirror Lake would become a dimmer reality for Olivia as she figured out how to navigate caring for Annabelle in the big city. And she would figure it out with flying colors, he had no doubt.

Maybe in some strange way he had taken Annabelle because part of him couldn't stop clinging to the fantasy of the three of them becoming a family.

Yet he'd expected Olivia to make all the compromises, adjust her life. He'd always thrown himself into whatever challenges he'd faced one hundred percent, but not this. And he'd lost her.

Maybe it was time to take his own advice. If it wasn't too late.

CHAPTER 19

"Liv, honey, you're not paying the least bit of attention. Would some sun-tea help? Julian just made some." Ryan Connor nodded to his longtime partner, who stood in their big open kitchen slicing lemons and dropping them into a glass pitcher.

"Oh, Ryan, I'm sorry." Olivia snapped out of her trance in time to pretend she'd been staring out the floor-to-ceiling windows of Ryan's oceanfront beach house instead of being lost in her own gray thoughts. "You invite me out to the Hamptons to get some work done and all I can do is drool at the view." From her seat on one of two pillowy white couches that resembled massive fluffy clouds, the ocean stretched endlessly in front of her, each little wave crested with a sparkling silver cap of sunlight.

Truthfully, she might as well have been looking out her apartment window at the brick wall of the building next door. Memories from the past few weeks both comforted and haunted her.

Like holding Annabelle as she snuggled in the crook of her arm, kissing her tiny soft toes, blowing on her tummy until she smiled. Who would have ever guessed that in such a short amount of time,

Annabelle had become a part of her, a deep and essential part, like a bone or a rib or a heart.

And so had Brad, who was cocky and cynical and loyal and the gentlest, most kind-hearted man she'd ever met. She saw him in that stupid grocery line, doling out paper towels as if they were his solution to world peace. After they'd made love, he'd held her hand over his heart like she was . . . precious. But was she? He loved Annabelle but as for her—had she simply been nothing other than his flavor of the month?

Lots of guys couldn't say the *L* word. And he'd warned her, he really had. But dammit, this time had seemed so different. She'd never felt like this before about anyone—except him when she was eighteen. Had it really been one-sided?

Ryan cast her a worried look. Despite working with him for the past year, only recently had they crossed the line from a strictly business relationship into friendship, and she was touched by his concern. "I'm fine. Really."

"You look exhausted."

She'd returned to her familiar, bustling life, with projects too numerous to fit into a day and not enough hours to sleep at night. Except when she did collapse into bed—and she waited until she was on the brink of exhaustion to avoid *thinking*—she couldn't sleep.

Every emotion was raw and on the surface. A baby's cry on the subway. An irritable toddler clinging to his mother after a too-long day. Small things she'd never even noticed before suddenly seemed magnified and personal.

Ryan raked a hand through his artfully spiky hair. Then he touched her hand, forcing her to look up from the screen. "You're upset over working like a dog all week, then I hauled your ass out here for the entire Memorial Day weekend."

Memorial Day weekend. A sudden, shooting stab of pain in her heart over and above the usual constant gnawing reminded her that

Bachelors Who Cook was tonight. At Brad's restaurant. And she was here, hours away, miserable without him.

Julian handed Olivia an ice-cold glass of cranberry-colored tea. "I'm warning you two," he said. "Tonight we're doing a clam bake on the beach, so you'd better kick it hard this afternoon so you can relax later. I'm not going to let this entire weekend pass with all work and no play."

Olivia smiled and sipped the tea. Ryan would easily work until midnight every night if it weren't for Julian.

Ryan flashed Julian a teasing smile. "You artists. Always so whimsical."

"Time for work and time for play, that's the key to balance, right, Mr. Assertiveness?"

Ryan laughed. "Ironic, isn't it? I write about helping people live full lives, yet I need someone to force me to slow down enough to enjoy my own."

"Well, you've got to or what kind of father will you be?" Julian teased.

"Father?" Olivia asked.

"Hasn't he told you?" Julian asked. "We're adopting twins."

Twin babies. Even as she congratulated them, longing for her own baby clutched at her heart.

She'd just thought of Annabelle as hers. *Her own baby.*

Olivia pressed her hands to her achy chest. Tried to breathe. Tears burned behind her eyes. How could she think of Annabelle as hers after so short a time? How had her heart expanded in ways she would never have thought possible?

"Are you all right?" Ryan grasped her shoulder. "Here, take another sip of tea."

Even as Olivia said "no, thank you" for the tea and reported she was *fine*, Annabelle's sweet little face appeared in front of her eyes.

Her heart squeezed so hard she felt a physical ache in her chest. She missed Annabelle. She missed being Annabelle's mother.

What she'd done seemed necessary. Ryan and Sylvia and an entire staff of people were counting on the completion of this project. Brad had stepped in and offered a solution and she'd taken it. Then why did she feel so awful?

She could have fought Sylvia. She could have had a heart-to-heart with Ryan. But for so many years, work was her number one priority, her only priority. The thing that drove her, made her feel like a success, and what kept the demons of a mother who'd abandoned her at bay.

But things had changed.

And now she had to, as well.

Maybe Brad didn't want her. Maybe he was all about Annabelle and providing her with a great life. He'd certainly let Olivia know that when she'd first come to town.

But maybe she never gave him a chance. She'd made it clear her home was here, in New York, but was it? She no longer found any solace in her silk blouses, her designer shoes, or her office's skyline view. Most of her friends seemed self-absorbed, totally into living a single's life.

Home now seemed to be the place where the people she loved lived. And it wasn't here. Not any more.

Ryan gathered up her hand and forced her to make eye contact. "All week I've been hoping you'd open up and share what happened when you went home, but you've seemed so upset. That's why I suggested we work here this weekend. You looked like you needed a break."

Olivia's eyes misted. He'd asked her out here for her own benefit, not just to work on the book. He was being a friend. But there was nothing he could do to help her.

Julian raised an assessing brow. "Maybe we need something stronger than tea." He headed back to the kitchen and returned with shot glasses, a box of tissues, and a bottle of Crown Royal. Olivia swiped at her eyes and laughed. "I must look like I need some *serious* intervention."

Ryan poured. "Because of you, this book is going to be bigger than *The Seven Habits of Highly Effective People*. I think it's time we become real friends, the kind that tell each other what's wrong."

"You wrote a spectacular book. It's going to help millions of people."

Ryan slid the shot glass across the fashionably battered table. "Spectacular because of your genius editing. Now drink up and confess. We're listening."

Olivia told them everything, about returning to Mirror Lake to take Annabelle, meeting Brad again, her struggles to learn how to care for the baby. She told them how she'd be nothing without her job, and how there didn't seem to be any compromise. She even told them how Bachelors Who Cook was going to be featured on an upcoming segment of Marc Daniels's Food Network cooking show.

Finally Julian spoke. "I have one question for you. You say he asked you to marry him."

"Under pressure. Without an *I love you*. Probably for Annabelle's sake."

"Is he the love of your life?"

"Yes." The word tumbled out without her even thinking. "Yes, he is," she found herself repeating slowly. "No one's ever made me feel like he does. But I can't go back to Mirror Lake without a job. My mother did that and it was . . . disastrous. Besides, my job is everything to me. Or at least it was. Since I've been back I haven't been able to concentrate on anything but Brad and Annabelle."

Julian and Ryan exchanged glances. Then Ryan spoke. "When we met, Julian owned a gallery in San Francisco. He couldn't imagine moving cross-country to a crowded city with a harsh winter."

Julian made a face. "I still abhor the crowds and the weather."

"But you did it anyway? For love?" Olivia asked, blowing her nose.

He nodded. "I bought a second gallery in New York. But even now, I travel back and forth. Since we bought this place, we spend every weekend here that we can. I don't feel that I gave up who I was to be with Ryan. You don't have to, either."

Ryan turned to speak to her. "The fact remains, you did an amazing job on my book. No one works as hard or demands such perfection, yet you deliver your demands with such a sweet smile I can't help but do what you say. Well, that and you're usually right." He laughed. "But Olivia, you're an accomplished editor. You've got resources and connections. If anyone can figure out how to make this work, you can."

Dammit, why couldn't she? For once in her life, why couldn't she step out of the confines of the box she'd caged herself into and insist on putting her own life first? She'd been so afraid of not making it, of not being something. So afraid to deviate from the straight and narrow lest she get lost in the woods. But in the process, she'd lost her identity. Or maybe she'd never given herself a chance to find out who she was. "I guess I've been afraid. I've been letting my past hold me back."

Ryan set his glass down with a smack on the glossy coffee table that looked molded from a tree stump. "Don't let fear stop you, honey. There's a whole chapter on that in the book, remember? You were the one who told me to leave it in."

"You're right. I am good at my job. But for the past ten years, that's all I've done, twenty-four seven, without questioning. I need a little time and space for my own life right now, and no one is going to make that happen but me."

"You go, girl. Take that space. Be assertive." Ryan turned to Julian. "Oh my God, this is so surreal. She's *living* my book. I'm absolutely *verklempt*."

"I *am* going to be assertive. Starting right now." Olivia stood and faced Ryan. "I want to finish editing the rest of your book remotely. There's no reason not to. Do you trust me to do that?"

Ryan stood and hugged her. "Honey, of course I do. I wish you would have said what was going on in the first place or I never would have insisted you come back."

"I won't make that mistake again." There were other mistakes she wished she hadn't made. Mistakes that might be too late to fix.

"It's so wondrous to see my book in action," Ryan said. "Maybe I'll use you as an example in the sequel."

"How do you know it's your book that's given her this sudden revelation?" Julian asked.

"Olivia?" Ryan looked at her expectantly.

"Okay, your book helped," Olivia said. "But it's mostly because of my sister."

"Your dead sister?" Ryan asked.

Olivia nodded. "Trish lived fully. She plunged into causes she believed in and every single day, she appreciated the people in her life. But it got cut short. She'll never get to see her dreams fulfilled or her baby grow into a beautiful young woman. What if I die? What will I have to show for a job I've slaved over for every waking hour for most of my twenties? So your book is right, Ryan. I have to take action instead of being a zombie, following along blindly in my own life. Things have to change, starting right now."

"Wow. That was really inspiring, Olivia," Julian said. "Maybe you should become a motivational speaker."

"Maybe I should have you write a few chapters of my next book," Ryan said.

Olivia laughed. "Yeah, I don't think you'd want that, since I'm more an example on how to do everything wrong." She'd poured her heart and soul into a job and forgot to live the rest of her life. She'd held her success like a banner above her head and waved it to everyone to prove she was worthy no matter what her mother had done to her. And worst of all, she'd used her job as an excuse to avoid intimacy with the one man she loved—whom she'd loved for most of her life.

Wasn't that the bottom line? Sticking to the well-known script of her life had been the perfect way to avoid getting her heart broken. Far less scary than taking a leap of faith. Maybe Brad was afraid of committing to a relationship. But maybe he, like herself, was just afraid of being abandoned.

Olivia glanced at her watch. Three o'clock. Bachelors Who Cook would begin at six. If she left now, she'd be pushing to get there in time to see Brad's big opening and bid on him as a bachelor. *Her* bachelor.

Because there was no way she was going to give him to Erika or any other woman. Not without a fight.

She cursed, remembering she'd taken the Jitney bus from the city and had no car. "I've got to get to Mirror Lake by six. Would either of you mind giving me a ride to a rental car place?"

Julian glanced at his Cartier watch then at Ryan. "Forget that. We'll take the Bentley. If we leave now we can make it."

"Just what I was thinking," Ryan said.

Olivia's eyes teared up as she grasped their hands. "I can't thank you enough."

"I was planning on watching Bachelors Who Cook," Ryan said with a chuckle. "Just not live."

CHAPTER 20

Thanks to Memorial Day traffic and merciless miles of road construction delays, when Brad finally pulled up to the marina, the cooking part of Bachelors Who Cook had already started. He strode quickly down the dock, past long tables covered with bright plastic tablecloths and serving pans heated with Sterno.

When Brad couldn't reach Olivia directly, he called her downtown Manhattan office and Sylvia had told him Olivia was working in the Hamptons for the weekend. He'd found Ryan Connor's beach house deserted. And he'd called Olivia's cell a million times to no avail. Finally, time was up. It was enough he'd left his staff in charge all day. He had to show up at the auction for the sake of the fundraiser.

The dock was crowded in the late afternoon heat, with people milling about tasting food and wine, laughing and talking. The scent of smoked ribs from a massive grill set up on the new deck of his restaurant filled the air. He waved to Philippe, who signaled him a thumbs-up. He was in his element, wearing a crisp white double-breasted chef jacket and toque as he worked the crowd.

Despite Brad's worries, everything had gone on just fine without him. Squinting in the bright sun, he searched all quadrants for a head of thick brown curls, a flash of deep brown eyes. But Olivia was nowhere.

He checked his cell again. *Nada.* And tried not to panic that he'd lost her for good.

Brad's brother, Ben, sat behind a table next to Olivia's father, surrounded by a crowd of young, tanned women in sundresses. Both guys appeared to be loving every minute. "Thanks for covering for me, Benjamin," Brad said, "but what's with all the napkins?" Ben clutched little scraps of paper that fluttered in the evening lake breeze.

"We ran out of lasagna rolls after a half hour. But the phone numbers just keep coming. Too fast to get them all in my phone." Ben grinned widely, anchoring the papers under a leg of the serving pan.

Tom stood nearby, tasting barbecued ribs and drinking beer out of a plastic cup. "I wanted to take your place but Alex said if I did, she'd castrate me."

"Where is Alex?" Brad asked, hoping he'd say "with Olivia". Because it *felt* like Olivia was here. His heart fired crazily, as revved as the engine on a Jaguar, every sense on alert. She *had* to be here. *Please, God, let her be here. Give me one last chance to get it right.*

But why wasn't she answering her phone?

Meg's approach interrupted their conversation. She was holding Annabelle, who wore a ruffly white dress with red polka dots and tiny blue sandals. Meg held out her hand, palm up, to Ben. "I can put those numbers in my purse for you if you'd like. Keep them safe."

"Thanks, Meggie." As Ben handed them over, the wind caught and blew them over the water.

"Hey!" he exclaimed, watching them flutter like ticker tape after a parade.

"Oops," Meg said, putting her fingers up to her mouth in mock surprise. Her tone would be called sassy if it was anyone but Meg. "So sorry about that."

Brad accosted Ben, who was still getting over the shock of losing all those numbers. "Ben, I was wondering if you'd take my place in the bachelor lineup tonight."

"Great idea, Brad." Meg turned to Ben. "You'll get plenty more floozies' numbers that way." Then she stalked off with Annabelle.

"Wonder what she's in a huff about," Ben said.

Brad shook his head. "For an ER doc, you're pretty clueless."

He didn't have time to elaborate. A female hand snaked around his arm. Brad spun, his breath catching. Just Erika, in a clingy leopard-print dress accentuating her big boobage. Holding a zipped-up dry cleaning bag. "Oh, my God, you're here," she cried on a deep sigh. "Where the hell have you been all day?"

"I had . . . urgent business." Still did. Where was Olivia?

"Ben *cannot* take your place. The whole town is cheering for you, for the restaurant. You've *got* to be part of the auction."

"I can't do it. I can't be auctioned off."

"Oh, yes, you can." Erika thrust the bag into his hand.

"What's in here?"

"Your tux," she huffed.

"Attention, everyone. Can I have your attention?" Everyone swung their gazes over to the brand new deck of Brad's restaurant, where a man with bright red skinny jeans, a yellow shirt, and hipster glasses held a microphone. He stood under a large banner that said *Bachelors Who Cook—for the Benefit of Mirror Lake Community Hospital*. "I'd like to call all of our cooking bachelors up here for the next part of our program."

"Who is that?" Brad asked.

"Marc Daniels cancelled, and that's his replacement. His name is Julian, he's an artist from New York, and he offered to help. Now go!" Erika gave him a shove that wasn't at all playful.

Julian's voice carried over the marina. "That famous chef, Marc Daniels, couldn't make it. I'm Julian Morris, your new MC. So come on up here, all you gorgeous bachelors!"

The crowd whooped and hollered. Everyone from town was there plus tons of foodies and tourists. The marina was jammed with boats, too, strung with strings of lights and flags in preparation for the big boat parade tonight.

No sign of Olivia. *Dammit,* she hadn't come after all. Disappointment prickled his insides—no, something far worse. Once, when he was in college, he'd driven through the plains states—Iowa, Nebraska, Kansas—through long stretches of flat land and frozen, waving grasses. It had been snowy and cold, the heater had been broken in his beat-up old car, and he'd never felt such desolation. He felt it now, despite the sunny eighty-degree day and the smell of great food and laughter spilling everywhere.

He'd lost her. The road ahead looked lonely and he was completely off course. And the last thing in the world that he wanted was to be fawned over by a bunch of young women flashing their cleavage and shiny white teeth and licking their glossy lips.

There was only one woman for him. Too bad she didn't want him.

He pulled out his phone one last time before he broke through the crowd. Nothing.

Brad changed in five minutes in the restaurant restroom. On the way out, Tom and Alex accosted him.

"Are you all right?" his brother asked.

Alex stepped forward to adjust his tie. "You look like hell." She actually spit on her hand and aimed to flatten his hair like he was one of her boys but he dodged. She got him anyway.

"I've been in New York all day."

Alex brushed lint off his jacket. "Tuck in your shirt."

"I can't find her. She wasn't there and she's not answering her phone."

"Get a grip, bro. She's here." Tom looked him in the eye, shook him by the shoulders, and gave him one last shove onto the deck, where a stage had been set up.

She's here. Tom's words echoed in Brad's ears as he half tumbled onto the makeshift stage. His heart galloped faster than a horse thundering into the final leg of the Preakness. He scanned the crowd, his gaze skimming back and forth over a sea of smiling faces.

Where was she? The faintest spark rekindled all his dashed hopes. He'd been given one last chance to fight for her. It would mean baring his soul to make it right and this time he wasn't holding back.

When Brad stepped up, everyone cheered, but he barely heard the noise. He stood next to the eleven other bachelors in evening wear and forced a smile, waving to Effie and Rosie and the boys and all the friends and neighbors he'd known for most of his life. But his eyes sought one woman, scanning the sea of faces tirelessly but coming up with—zero.

Julian herded the men together. "Okay, everyone. We're here to raise some money for the hospital, so come on, ladies, dig down deep in your pockets to bid on these hot guys. Top bidder wins a date with the bachelor, and the guy who goes for the most money gets to be on the cover of *Connecticut Foodie Magazine*. So, let's go!"

The bidding began. Heat gathered under Brad's collar and he yanked it to loosen it a little. He kept a smile painted on his face, but inside he was dying.

And then his cell phone buzzed.

Pulling it from his pocket, he read his text. The most precious two words of his life.

I'm here.

⊢·◆◇·○·◇◆·⊣

People pressed from all sides and Olivia felt her hair starting to spring out wildly in the humidity despite the gallon of hairspray her friends had generously applied. Sweat beaded on her lip and her pretty dress stuck to her skin.

It was a black chiffon halter dress, a reject Alex had found in the stock room from an all-black wedding. She'd taken shears and mercilessly whacked off the large red satin flower that had been sewn onto the waist-line so it now looked slightly less wedding-ish. The shoes were strappy black sandals that Meg had pulled from her own closet. Who suspected that Meg even *owned* fuck-me shoes?

In Olivia's haste, she'd forgotten her phone in New York but now she held Meg's. She jumped up and down, waved her hands, trying to attract Brad's attention while she slogged through the sticky bodies to the stage. She had to get to him before it was too late. Before every single woman went wild over him.

Julian's voice boomed over the mike. "We're going to start the bidding on our most popular bachelor, hometown son, entrepreneur, benefactor of many Mirror Lake charities . . . Mr. Brad Rushford!"

Sweat rolled down her back as Olivia flung herself through the tangle of arms and legs, children eating hot dogs and cotton candy, and toddlers clinging to their parents' legs.

The crowd clapped as Brad took the mike.

"Olivia. Olivia, where are you?" Brad's voice echoed along the lakefront as he looked about.

Olivia's muscles froze in place. *Oh my God, did he just say my name? Out loud? Or am I hallucinating?*

Everyone hushed, sensing something extraordinary was happening.

"I'm here!" she yelled as loud as she could. She pushed forward, waving her arms wildly. "Right here!"

This time, the bodies parted. Not only that, but a thousand eye-balls turned to stare at her. A buzz tore through the marina.

Brad finally caught her gaze and held out his arm. "Come up here, sweetheart. Come up here right now."

She locked her eyes on gorgeous, handsome Brad, in a slim-fit tux, looking like the one and only man she'd ever loved in her life. He was there, waiting for her, his worried gaze fixed on her, only her. As if the thousand people surrounding them didn't exist.

Behind him, the sun was setting over the pier, an orange ball of fire in a smoky blue sky. How many times had she seen that same sun set over this old town? Except that now its beauty seemed precious to her. The sunset blurred in a haze of sudden tears. All she could see as she blinked them back was Brad, center stage, taking the mike to speak.

"I'm Brad Rushford, owner of Reflections, sponsor of this event, and I just wanted to say a word. Is that okay?"

"Say away," Julian said, stepping back.

"First, I wanted to thank everyone for coming out today. The Bachelors Who Cooked, I wanted to thank them, too. The event was a big success. And tonight, our auction is for a great cause."

Amid the applause, Brad handed the mike back to Julian. Whispered something in his ear.

"But we're in the middle of auctioning you off," Julian said, his voice a little panicked. "What am I supposed to do with this crowd?" Realizing he'd accidentally announced that into the mike, Julian's face turned the color of the setting sun.

Brad, grinning, patted him on the back, then dashed to the edge of the stage. His gaze singled out Olivia and fixed on her like a tractor beam as she pushed through the last few rows of bodies.

Julian faced the throng gamely. "Okay, party people. Our auction has been delayed for a few minutes while our bachelor takes care of some . . . business. I know Marc Daniels couldn't make it, but we have a real celebrity in our midst who I know would love to give you some tips this Memorial Day weekend on being assertive. Let's have a big hand for *New York Times* best-selling author, Ryan Connor!"

Everyone went with it and roared.

Ryan stepped up to the stage and hugged his partner.

"Thanks, Julian." He beamed at the masses before him. "Let's take a few moments to talk about working hard to get what you want."

CHAPTER 21

When Olivia finally reached the makeshift stage, Brad grasped her hands and lifted her up the stairs as if she weighed as much as a ball of cotton. He wasted no time crushing her to him. "You're here." Emotion weighed down his voice.

Engulfed in his arms, she breathed in the scent of him, familiar and wonderful. She was home at last.

"I had to see you," she whispered. "Nothing's been the same since I left."

"I went to New York to find you but you were gone. And you weren't answering your cell."

"I accidentally left it at my apartment."

He caressed her face. His startling green eyes blazed with intensity. Passion. Relief. "I love you," he said, his voice breaking. "I've decided to start a new restaurant in New York. Hell, I'll open one in Siberia if that's what it takes to have you."

Her heart stuttered as a big, blooming chunk of hope took hold in her chest and clung. "You mean Annabelle's not your number-one concern?" she choked out. She touched his hair, his cheek, making sure he was real. That *this* was real.

"I love Kevin's child with my whole heart and I would give up my own life to protect her. But what I feel for you"—he took a deep breath—"what I feel for you is more than I can even express. I was afraid to say it, afraid you'd leave again and not look back. But I love you, Olivia. I can't imagine a life without you and Annabelle."

The precious words misted her eyes. All the joy in her heart prepared to flood out. Except there was just one last thing. "I thought you didn't want to raise any more kids."

Brad's gaze, bright with emotion, drilled directly through her. Set her to trembling, but his hold on her was unrelenting. "I'd be lying if I told you it didn't still scare me. But my sister made me realize that maybe I've been so afraid of screwing up that I forgot to notice what I did right. No one can predict the future, but I can guarantee one thing. Our children will be loved, Olivia. We can share all the ups and downs together."

"No."

He quirked a brow. "No?"

"No, I don't want you to move to New York." She took a deep breath and plunged in. "These past few weeks have taught me I'm not my mother. And being in New York made me recognize I'm not my job, either. So I've decided to do something a little different. Going through this experience has made me realize there aren't any books out there for people who suddenly become parents, like I did, with little notice. So I was thinking I could write one. It's going to be full of resources and advice—as soon as I learn it all myself."

A tiny smile played at the corners of his mouth. "You're going to write a self-help book instead of edit one."

"And I want to live right here, in Mirror Lake, with our family and friends."

"Won't you miss the City?"

She shook her head. "Home is where you are, Brad.' Besides, it's close enough that I can go back and forth when I need to."

He dropped to one knee, and this time he looked her straight in the eye. Her limbs went numb with shock. Blood heated her cheeks and her heart pounded so loud she was afraid she would miss the question. She was vaguely aware that Ryan had stopped talking, of the sudden silence of a thousand people waiting on bated breath with her.

"Marry me, Olivia."

She nodded, tears blurring her vision. Brad stood and pulled her tight against him, planted his lips firmly over hers. She wrapped her arms around his neck and gave it back with all she had.

The crowd went wild.

He murmured something in her ear. Drew away, groped in his jacket pockets.

"What is it?" she asked.

"Dammit, it's in my other pants pocket . . ."

She tugged on his arm to get him to look at her. "I don't need that now."

A huge smile spread over Brad's handsome face as he gathered her back into his arms and looked deeply into her eyes. "I loved you a long time ago, I love you now, and I'll love you forever."

All she could see of his face was a huge watery blur. But she felt his strength surround her, smelled his warm cologne and sunshine scent carried on the familiar lake breeze. "I've always loved you, Brad. I always will."

Cheers exploded all around them. Meg walked up and handed Annabelle to her, and Olivia kissed and hugged the tiny baby she would love as her own forever.

Ryan finally took the mike. "Brad Rushford, you're officially disqualified from Bachelors Who Cook."

Brad gave a *who, me?* shrug of innocence.

"You want to know why? Because you've just revoked your bachelorhood!"

Amid more cheers and more than a few disappointed *boos,* Brad leaned toward the mike. "I want to call a substitute." His gaze flicked through the masses of people. "Frank Marks, get up here."

Somehow, amidst all the commotion, Brad helped Olivia and the baby down and Alex and Tom steered the three of them to a quiet spot near the restaurant. Effie had tears in her eyes. Olivia kissed her and handed her Annabelle to hold.

Then she hugged Alex and Meg. "Thank you both for helping me."

Alex, the softie that she was, was full-out bawling. As she dabbed at her eyes with a Kleenex, she pointed at the stage. "Oh my gosh, your father's up there. He's about to be auctioned off."

>⊶⊙⊷⊰

Later that night, Brad and Olivia gathered at Alex and Tom's house with the rest of the family to watch the 11:00 p.m. news coverage of the event.

Samantha walked in just before eleven, looking flustered, and made her way to Olivia and Annabelle on the couch. "My cell battery died so I was checking my e-mail on Trish and Kevin's computer, and when the e-mail came up, it was still logged in to Trish's account. I hope you don't mind, but I copied these for you. It's from a couple weeks before the accident."

She handed Olivia a page of cut-and-pasted e-mails. The first heading said *RE: The Will.* Her sister's own words blurred in front of her. Olivia's hands shook as she stared blankly at the paper.

Brad, who was sitting next to her, wrapped a strong arm around her and the baby. He gave a small nod. As she searched his soft green eyes, she somehow found the courage to read.

> *I want us to name Olivia as Annabelle's guardian. Tom and Alex are busy with all their own kids, Samantha's too young, and Brad's already raised the whole bunch of you.*

Kevin's reply was next.

You sure she'll go for that? She doesn't exactly have time for a kid.

Olivia looked up. She couldn't go on. Seeing the words in print was too much.

"Keep reading," Brad urged in a soft voice.

"I . . . can't." Olivia silently pleaded for his strength.

Brad gently extracted the pages from her hands. "Trish wrote, *'You don't know my sister like I do. She protected me from bullies, taught me about my period, and chased away Robbie Perkins when he started stalking me in high school. She gave me the sex talk when my dad was too embarrassed, and she told me to go straight through and get my master's in library science because I'd have better opportunities and better pay, even if I planned to stay in Mirror Lake. I want Annabelle to grow up strong and determined and fearless, like my sister.'"*

Olivia closed her eyes, shook her head slowly. Unbelievable. Trish's parting gift to her. She'd known all along what Olivia had to learn on her own.

Everyone was sniffling. Meg was sobbing outright. Samantha and Alex hugged. Even Tom pinched his nose and Ben shifted his gaze uncomfortably downward.

Brad gathered Olivia into his big arms, kissed her head and Annabelle's sleepy one. "She wanted you to be the one all along." His eyes shone with love and Olivia knew at that moment that she was exactly where she was meant to be. "Took me a little longer to be as convinced," he said with a wry grin.

"You came around eventually," Olivia said. "'Course, I could convince you about my loving side a little later if you're unsure."

"Sweetheart, you can demonstrate that any time you want."

"Told you so," Effie said, wiping her own tears. "But it's eleven o'clock and time to stop all the bawling. The news is on." She clicked on the remote.

The male anchor announced the big local story of the day. Suddenly, the camera cut to tape of Erika at the lakefront interviewing people in the crowd.

"That's your father," Alex exclaimed.

"How does it feel to be the bachelor who went for the highest price, Frank?" Erika asked, then pushed the mike in front of Olivia's dad's face.

Olivia looked at Brad, pure shock jolting her. "The highest price? My *dad*?"

"Your dad?" Brad echoed in disbelief.

Ben chuckled quietly. "Told you those were some lasagna rolls."

The camera panned to a woman next to Frank. Jeannie Marshall grinned widely and linked arms with his. Frank shot her an adoring look and patted her hand.

"Jeannie's been sweet on your dad for quite a while," Brad said. "It's about time those two got together."

Jeannie Marshall and her *dad*? Well, why not. He probably would enjoy a little house on the lake with a nice screened porch if he could share it with her.

Olivia's father spoke into the microphone. "I couldn't be more thrilled . . . to make this event a real success for Mirror Lake Community Hospital, that is."

"That sounds humble, like my dad," Olivia said.

"Oh, hell," Frank continued, "I'm pretty darn thrilled about you picking me, too, Jeannie." Then he puckered up and kissed her, right on national TV.

"Oh my God," Olivia said.

"Well, who knew Frank had it in him," Tom said.

"Oh, he had it in him," Brad said. "He just needed a good woman to bring it out." He flashed Olivia that killer smile that never failed to send her stomach pitching. Then he kissed her good and hard in front of the whole family.

EPILOGUE

On a fine midsummer day, Olivia stood in line at the grocery story checking off her list. And blowing air kisses to Annabelle, who beamed radiant smiles at everyone in line from her perch in her baby carrier snuggled against Brad's chest.

"Such a beautiful baby," an elderly lady behind them said, clasping her hands together in exclamation.

"And so well behaved," her husband added.

"She's the best." Olivia turned and smiled at Brad.

Brad grinned broadly and winked. "She hardly ever cries."

"You two lovebirds are next," Gertie said a little too loudly from behind the cash register. Olivia wheeled the cart forward while Brad unloaded the groceries.

Gertie slid crabmeat, garlic, olive oil, and panko breadcrumbs through the scanner. She pulled up the rhinestone-jaded reading glasses from the chain around her neck and squinted at a small box. "*Quin-oh-ah*. What has the world come to? Eating food I can't even pronounce."

"Don't worry, Gertie," Olivia said. "I can't cook it either."

"Leave that to me. But I see you've planned dessert." Brad extracted a roll of refrigerated cookie dough hidden under fresh asparagus stalks and waved it in the air.

Olivia snagged her dough back from Brad. "So my cooking skills need a little work."

"That's okay." He leaned close to her ear. "You have other talents that make up for it."

"My goodness, look how this little lady has grown." Gertie tickled Annabelle's tiny foot while the baby sucked on a rattle and quietly assessed Gertie. "You're not sharing space with the groceries today, are you, little girl?" Annabelle kicked and grinned, dropping the rattle, clearly relieved not to have a two-liter of diet cola wedged next to her elbows.

"So when's the wedding?" Gertie asked.

Olivia bent to retrieve the toy. "We've got the church secured for Labor Day weekend. Now we just need a place for the reception. Got any ideas?"

"How about the yard of that old Victorian?" Mike Rossi stood in line a few people behind them, holding a take-out salad and a packet of dressing.

Brad stiffened and sent Mike a warning shake of his head.

What was going on?

Mike rambled on, clearly nonplussed by Brad's ominous looks. "By the way, I had the roof inspected. And it's going to cost you to replace it with authentic slate. Not to mention the gutters are plugged and half of them aren't even connected anymore."

Olivia froze, head of lettuce in hand. "You had the roof inspected? And the gutters?"

"That house sold," Brad said quickly.

"It sold." Olivia couldn't believe it. "But why did you . . ."

Brad's eyes gleamed with mischief, and the corner of his mouth turned up in a wicked grin. "Yeah, some couple with a baby bought it."

"Oh." She couldn't help the tiny swell of disappointment that surfaced. But it was, after all, only a house, so she shrugged. "At least a young family got it."

"We can move in right after we're married. If Mike gets all that work done on time, right, Mike?"

Olivia dropped the lettuce into the cart. "You *bought* it? For us?"

He was never one to blush, but ruddy color infused his cheeks. "Yeah, I did."

She squeezed past the cart and threw her arms around him, showering kisses all over his face. "I love that house almost as much as I love you two."

"It needs a lot of work."

She kissed Annabelle on the forehead, relished her sweet baby scent. "Did you hear that, Annabelle? You're going to have a great big yard where you can chase your dog."

"Not to mention all her other brothers and sisters," Brad said.

Olivia beamed. "Maybe a nice fat cat, too."

Brad turned around in the line. "Mike, did you not remember I asked for your confidence?"

"You are confident in me, Brad. I'm the best damn restoration specialist in town. I can't help it you bought a giant squatting white elephant." He rubbed his hand on his neck. "It will be beautiful one day . . . but it'll cost you."

"Okay, folks, thanks for all the PDA but it's time to get the line moving." Gertie held out a small box. "Don't forget your tea candles. Somehow, I think they're going to come to good use with that romantic dinner."

"Who needs dinner?" Brad said in a low voice, holding Olivia close as he pushed out the cart.

"I have a great idea for dessert," Olivia whispered. "And I'm not talking about fresh-baked cookies."

She followed as Brad steered the cart out toward the door. What a couple of weeks it had been, and it had taught her a lot of lessons. How life could turn on a dime and shake up your whole world in ways you never imagined. How you could go home again even if you thought you couldn't. How a tragedy could make you discover the love of your life again in the least likely place.

Her heart full of gratefulness, Olivia reached up on tiptoe to graze Brad's lips.

They were warm and sweet and held the promise of many more kisses as they walked together through the years of their lives.

"Let's take our little girl out of here," Brad said, wrapping an arm around Olivia's shoulders. Then the family headed together toward home.

ACKNOWLEDGMENTS

I used to think that writing was done in a vacuum. How wrong I was! There are so many people to thank in helping with the birth of this baby.

Finding Romance Writers of America has plugged me into valuable resources I would never have found otherwise. My sisters at Northeast Ohio RWA and the talented women of the Sunshine critique group—Chris Anna, Mary, Sheri, Vicki, and Wendy—have been a constant source of encouragement and support. My Lucky 13 Golden Heart sisters are there daily to share the ups and downs of being a writer. I love you all.

Thanks to Lori Wilde, who in her novel writing class taught me how to put together a story, starting with how to write a scene. You saw the earliest starts of this story and helped it make sense.

Thanks to my agent, Jill Marsal, who is hardworking and dedicated. You taught me many things about how to write a story that sells. I'm not sure what you saw in that first scary draft, but I'm so glad you did see it!

To Maria Gomez, who was enthusiastic about this book from the beginning and welcomed me to the Montlake family. To Charlotte Herscher, whose editorial insights went deep into the psyches of my characters and greatly enriched the book.

To my husband, who always treats my characters like real people and troubleshoots their dilemmas like he takes on all other problems in life . . . with great gusto and a sense of humor that makes me laugh no matter how impossible the situation.

To my kids, who learned a long time ago to tolerate disarray and even relish it. Your support means everything to me. I wish for you to follow your dreams and never settle for less than true love.

To my mom and dad, who loved me unconditionally and always taught me to do my best. I hope there are Kindles in heaven.

And lastly, thanks to my readers. Especially every woman who has had to make tough decisions about her career and her children. Like my heroine, you are all super women.

ABOUT THE AUTHOR

Miranda Liasson loves to write stories about courageous but flawed characters who find love despite themselves, because there's nothing like a great love story! In addition to *This Thing Called Love*, which won the 2013 Golden Heart for Series Romance, she writes contemporary category romance for Entangled Publishing. She lives in the Midwest with her husband, three kids, and office mates Maggie, a yellow lab, and Posey, a rescue cat with attitude.

Made in the USA
Middletown, DE
16 February 2019